SKRELSAGA

 www.trafford.com

North America & international
toll-free: 1 888 232 4444 (USA & Canada)
fax: 812 355 4082

**Acknowledgements**

To Bruce Dent, for reading an early draft and letting me know that I hadn't wasted my time.

To Delwyn Klassen, for some great editing and amazing artwork.

To Mum and Dad, for financing.

To Gan and Bruno, for knowing when it's a good time to stop writing and go for a walk.

A Note on Skrel Pronunciation &
Naming

The Skrel language should pose no problems with pronunciation, with a few exceptions.

>*dd* as in *th*en
>*w* as in b*oo*k, except where following a vowel
>*y* where on its own, or before a consonant as *uh*

Skrel are given their first names at birth, *Grok, Leku* and so on. The rest of their name follows around 12 to 15 years later.
Names can be as simple as son of, *al* or daughter of, *el.*
A Skrel can be identified by his home, if he has spent time away, e.g. *Gron ar Tolgath.*
Another possibility is the Skrel's profession, *Lwd y Relddu* is a blacksmith.
The final source is descriptive of the Skrel him or herself, as with *Grok y Gremnor,* the wanderer.
The final choice of name is made by the young Skrel and they keep that name. Female Skrel do not change their names on marrying

Chapter I

Grok was sitting close to the fire. Even his furs and hooded cloak seemed no protection against the chill wind that blew down from the Haramor Mountains. He had been in colder temperatures in his mountainous homeland, but this wind seemed maliciously cold. There was still another day's travel before he reached Alghol.

In the darkness beyond the firelight he saw a shape moving. It looked human. He called to it.

"Come and share the warmth if you want! What there is!"

The figure slowed its walk and turned as the bass voice hailed it, then moved towards the fire. It was also wearing a hooded cloak and supported itself with a staff. Its voice was that of an old man.

"Thank you. It is a cold night for travel, but travel I must and I fear the next inn is further than I had thought." It paused. "You are heading for Alghol?"

"Yes," Grok replied as the figure slowly sat down opposite him.

"That is no great surprise in these parts. I am travelling to that city myself. My name is Calon Gan."

"Grok." He threw back his hood. "Of the Skrel."

The old man regarded him from under his hood. He saw the coarse hair and beard, the large fangs and the piercing eyes shining in the firelight. The whole visage a picture of the human term 'monstrous'.

"I have no fear of your race," the old man said. "I once knew a skrel called Krarg."

"You knew Krarg?" rumbled Grok, pulling his hood

back up.

"Many years ago. More than I care to remember. I know also the history of your race."

There was a silence for some time.

"Why is a skrel here in the land of Erein?"

"Why are you here?"

"A question for a question. Well said my young friend. I am one of the Order of Freidyn. One of the few left."

"I am a traveller."

"This is still a good time to be a traveller, but for how long I cannot say. You would do well to travel north, back to Skrelbard."

"Not yet, but soon," growled Grok.

"In the meantime, perhaps you will accompany me to Alghol. There are some who have no respect for age, yet much for your considerable strength."

Grok considered. The old man claimed to have known Krarg. He nodded.

"Thank you. Solitary travel, whilst sometimes welcome, can be difficult at times."

There was a further silence, which suited Grok. Never the most talkative of skrel, his taciturn nature hid an intelligent mind. That and his Skrellian physique usually led humans and elves to underestimate him to their severe disadvantage.

On the other side of the fire, Calon Gan was considering matters. He settled himself more comfortably and decided that he would have to break the silence.

"You are not the first skrel I have heard of here and in Corbus," he began.

"There are many of us on Skrelbard, some travel far from home before they return," Grok rumbled.

"You are not known as travellers, though you trade with people in the north," Calon Gan persisted.

The Skrel's shining eyes fixed on the old man's face for a moment before Grok began speaking. "We know that humans think of skrel when they talk of fearsome monsters. We hear some of the old stories you tell your children, which they tell their children." Calon Gan shifted slightly. Grok's tone was level as he stated the facts, which was more discomforting than anger. "The elves and barances can live among humans, yet my people do not because they are often not welcomed."

"Some of us are more welcoming," Calon Gan replied. "Too often, people do not look beyond the surface of things and fear what they do not know. Before I travelled to Skrelbard the most people could tell me of the skrel was you were good drinking partners and terrible enemies."

Grok laughed as his companion stopped talking. "There is more than surface to all things."

"Truly said my friend. The libraries of the Freidyn hold many stories of the past and they speak of the Skrel. One scribe wrote of a terrible secret on Skrelbard that your people will never reveal."

"Do you believe him?" Grok asked, with a sharper tone in his voice.

"He presented it as a piece of an old tale. I have no reason to believe it is otherwise." He paused as Grok growled under his breath. "My experience with skrel leads me to believe you are a tolerant and amiable race. Still, I know better than to generalise an entire people."

"You show sense. What do you think of me?"

Calon Gan saw the quick flash of a grin cross Grok's face as he asked the question. "You are a robust representative of your race and certainly amiable enough to share your fire. There is danger in joining a companion on the road yet I feel I have chosen wisely." Calon Gan closed his eyes as a wave of tiredness swept over him.

Grok noticed the old man's reaction, "You should rest now."

"Mine is a journey for a younger man, yet there is none to take it."

"Then you must rest when you can."

"With age comes wisdom, yet also aches, pains and many problems. Thank you, Grok."

Calon Gan wrapped his cloak tighter around himself and lay down near the fire. Grok looked at him, wondering what quest brought such a man out on this journey. He yawned as he put some more wood on the fire. Snagging a length of string around his wrist he made himself comfortable on the ground and relaxed. The other end of the string was attached to his backpack and acted as security for his possessions. Like Grok it was easily underestimated. Although seemingly easy to cut, it would resist the sharpest knife.

Hours later, in the darkest portion of the night a cowled figure passed the camp. Its garments were so dark it almost disappeared in the shadows as it glanced at the sleeping figures in the firelight, before switching its attention to a stealthy silhouette approaching Calon Gan. The cowled figure softly spoke a name and the other fell to the ground with a faint groan.

The cowled figure paused to consider matters. There was potential for much work ahead. The Skrel and the Freidyn could make his task easier. Even so, he should take a break. A day off wouldn't affect things much. Maybe a day on the coast. As the figure moved off, musing about a day by the sea, its cloak brushed Grok. The Skrel immediately awoke and reached for the axe strapped to his backpack. He scanned the area, but he perceived no threat. After many minutes he returned to sleep.

Grok was heating water as the sun rose. Fortunately, it did not rise early this time of year. As the pot came to a boil he wondered if he would be in Skrelbard for Tolfast. The days of feasting and fun were something to be enjoyed with friends.

Calon Gan woke and observed Grok at the fire. "Good morning."

Grok growled a greeting in return, hoping that the old man would not be too cheerful. Calon Gan slowly got to his feet and began to walk to the trees. He called to Grok, "There's a body here!"

Grok walked over to see. It was a middle aged man in dark clothes and carrying a dagger. There were no obvious signs of injury.

"Did you do this?" Gan asked.

"No. I was aware of something in the night, but that was not a human." He relapsed into silence and moved back to the fire.

When the water had boiled he made *cwr* and passed a cup to Calon Gan. The old man accepted the hot drink and offered him some bread in return and they completed the meal with dried meat from Grok's pack.

Breakfast over and the fire extinguished, Grok improvised a shovel and dug a shallow grave for the corpse they had found. Then, the mismatched pair set off for Alghol. There were other travellers on the road, some in carts and others on foot. Some stopped to exchange information and passed on the news of robbers being seen further up the road. Grok walked with his hood down as the sun warmed the land. Perhaps that was why they were unmolested. There was very little talk during the journey.

"Do you know Alghol well?" Calon Gan asked after an hour or so.

"No," replied Grok.

"Is there someone there who we should report that man's death to?" the old man tried again, after it became clear that Grok was not going to speak.

"We do not know who he is, we buried him. What can we tell people?" Grok replied.

"It would seem so. Where do you plan to stay in Alghol? I would like to repay your hospitality of last night."

"There is no need," Grok growled.

Calon Gan devoted his energy to keeping pace with the Skrel and abandoned his attempts at conversation. Grok continued to walk in silence. He had talked last night to learn about the old man and, having formed an opinion, was content to stay silent.

When they neared Alghol, Grok once more raised his hood. There were more people on the road and a few glanced at the old man and the large hooded figure next to him. Travellers were more frequent as they reached the fork where the road to Execrul branched to the south. Clouds had built up during the journey and now snow began to fall.

The Skrel walked with Gan as far as the house where Luden Kul lived .

"Thank you for your company," said Gan.

"Not a problem," rumbled Grok and set off down the street. Gan watched him for a moment, then turned to the door and knocked.

Chapter II

A short time later he was talking to Luden Kul.

"Thank you for coming, Calon."

"A request from you is not to be lightly refused, Luden."

"There are few of us left. I would not have chosen to bring you so far if it were not necessary."

"Your messenger said that it was urgent."

"Were you aware that a number of skrel are travelling here and in Corbus?"

"Yes, I have just been travelling with one."

"It may be that the skrel will be the most important race very soon." Gan looked at him inquiringly. "A long time ago the Freidyn used their power to foresee timelines. They kept records of what they saw. Some of them were proved to be accurate. This is nearly as far as they looked, for reasons no longer understood. It may be that their powers had a finite reach. There were two alternatives recorded in their journals. In one, things continued much as they are. In the other was widespread destruction and death. The skrel seemed to be the key. I want you to travel to Skrelbard. There may be something happening there that will give us the key to the situation."

"That will be possible."

"Can you find the Skrel you travelled with?"

"I believe so."

"If he is travelling to Skrelbard, go with him. Out of all of us, you have the most experience with the skrel. If he is not, then I would ask you to travel there yourself and investigate. The amount of magic required to foresee the future is beyond our means. We must use the resources we have without magic."

Magic was occasionally used as a tool, for sending messages long distances especially. But old stories told of mages who could move mountains, or at least make them change colour. History seemed to be rich in magic, but it had faded over the years. If a mage tried to turn a mountain red these days, he would be doing well to turn a few boulders slightly pink. The occasional mage capable of stronger spells tended to die young, their own energy drained by the spells they cast.

Some time later Calon Gan had walked to the area

of the city known as Kelno. Luden Kul had told him of a skrel family there who acted as trade ambassadors and suggested they might know of the traveller's whereabouts.

Calon Gan entered a tavern to make enquiries and saw a well-built figure at a table. It was facing away from him, but the coarse hair and lupine ears showed it to be a skrel. Since it would be the best one to ask about skrel, Gan crossed the room towards it . As he neared the figure, he saw that it was Grok.

"Fortune smiles on us, my friend. You are the one I am seeking."

"Really?"

"I have been speaking to a senior member of my order. He has asked me to travel to Skrelbard."

"Why?"

"For reasons that may be vitally important or may be unimportant. At this moment it is impossible to say which is true."

"You are looking for me because...?"

"I require a travelling companion. As I have a high opinion of you and you did suggest you were travelling to Skrelbard, I would choose to travel with you."

Grok drank some more beer to increase the time before he answered. This character hadn't been any trouble on the way to Alghol and he was leaving for the island soon. He planned to travel overland to Grimsbal and then by boat to Tromok. From there would be a short journey to Tolgath.

He told Gan of his plan and the old man agreed with it. They agreed to meet about an hour after sunrise and the old man left to return to Luden Kul's house.

Grok was left alone. He finished the food on the table and continued drinking beer and thinking. After some time another skrel entered the tavern and joined him.

"Grok, it has been a long time," he said, sitting down.

"How are your family?" Grok asked, as a tankards of beer were placed between them.

"They are well," Lucras answered, handing over money for the drinks. "What news from you?"

"The Council has not reformed and I have the Stone of Erypmon."

"That is good. Where is it?"

Grok searched through his many pockets before producing a small, reddish, oval-shaped stone with letters carved on it. Lucras examined it.

"To think that this stone broke the barriers to the Outer Darkness. What are we doing with it?"

Grok took back the stone and dropped it into a different pocket.

"I will give it to Friy in Tromok. His forge will destroy it."

"If they try to return it will delay them. But it might not stop them. I may return to Skrelbard myself."

Grok looked at him. "The last stand?"

"If it should be necessary. We both know what the fall of Skrelbard will mean."

There was a brief silence.

"I'm at a house on Knoll Street, the one with *Croesen* written on the door." Lucras continued. "I will see you for dinner later."

Left alone once more Grok continued drinking his beer. After some time he moved to his room on the floor above. He crossed to the window and looked at the snow falling in the gathering darkness. Below, people were hurrying through the flakes. Trying to get home before the darkness came.

Turning his attention to his backpack, he formed a small package that matched the size and weight of the Stone. He hid the package under the lumpy mattress and left the room. His circuitous route about the city eventually led to Knoll Street and the home of Lucras' family.

Some hours later when he returned to the room he checked the package. It was still in place and untouched, he took it from under the mattress and placed it in his backpack. So, no one knew about it, he reflected as he did so.

The following morning saw Grok waiting at the old North Gate with what seemed to the Algholians to be a menacing air. It was merely a combination of Skrellian physique and waiting for his morning *cwr* to kick in. Still, it left an area around him free of people which he appreciated.

He hadn't been waiting long when Calon Gan arrived. Grok noted approvingly that he was wearing clothes suitable for the weather in Skrelbard.

"Good morning. I trust you slept well."

"Not bad," Grok rumbled. "Are you ready?"

"I am. Lead on to Grimsbal."

They passed through the gate and into what the

Algholians called the wildlands and Grok thought of as a nice place to live. There was little conversation during the journey. Calon Gan was content with his own thoughts, knowing it was easier than getting conversation out of his large companion.

It was four days journey to Grimsbal over a lightly used track. After passing through Jorvak they were able to join others on an open cart which made the journey to Grimsbal occasionally. On arrival they secured passage on a boat leaving the following day. The boat's captain recommended an inn to them and they walked there in the dark. The people of Grimsbal were used to travellers and a skrel with a human caused no comment. They found rooms and later ate together.

"It is near Tolfast, I think." Calon Gan said, after their meal.

Grok confirmed it was.

"I should like to attend a feast again. Though I fear that I cannot eat and drink as much as I did last time."

Grok was silent for a moment. "I will be hosting the Eenfast in Tolgath. You will be welcome to join us."

"Thank you. I will look forward to it."

A longer pause. Grok continued drinking beer as Gan sipped at mulled wine.

"I believe Krarg had a son."

"Thenk."

"He was but a youngster the last time I saw him, many years ago. Do you know anything of him these days?"

"He will be in Tolgath."

"I would like to speak to him, I have many

questions for the skrel."

"Yet you do not ask me."

"I mean no insult, yet I feel that you would not answer them."

"These are days where it is not safe to share all knowledge."

"I fear that you are correct," Calon Gan sighed and finished his wine. "I will see you in the morning, good night."

"Sleep well."

Grok remained alone, watching the patrons of the inn. His attention was caught by a stranger in a black hooded cloak. What could be discerned was that it was a male, either a lightly built human or an elf. The voice was hoarse, Grok caught the words, " Drek Tarl..... Monstrea". He knew that the places were far to the south and the dark relevance they had held, centuries ago when some of the mage guilds used those places to pierce the barriers and bring creatures into the world from the Darknesses. Guilds that were allied to the Council of Barakelth and assisted their twisted schemes. Draining his tankard, Grok moved to the bar for more beer and passed close to the hooded figure. A glimpse of the face showed it to be human, they were now discussing the chances of bad weather for a sea voyage. Grok took his beer back to where he had been sitting, the inn was too quiet for him to move closer unobserved. There may have been an innocent explanation but the mention of Monstrea had worried him. The two seemed to be continuing their conversation but after Grok had returned from the outhouse they were both gone. Deciding that asking the innkeeper about his customers would not help, Grok went to his room.

The following morning, after a large breakfast, Grok and Calon Gan left the inn for the boat. The wind had changed direction in the night and blew from the north, bringing the cold from the snowfields of Skrelbard. The snow that had begun to melt in the warm weather froze again leaving the streets slippery.

There were only four other passengers on the ship. With a favourable wind the journey could be done in three days but the master was dubious about the possibility of less than five for this trip. Apart from a skrel named Kalt, the passengers were traders. There was a small trade in furs from Skrelbard. Skrel-brewed mead sold far and wide and some Skrel carvings and pottery had a good reputation to the south. Some skrel brought in cloth and there was a trade in spices from far over the Morfawr. The northern centre for spices was Grimsbal and spice traders would travel from there to Tromok. The sea could be treacherous in the winter and the only fast travel in Skrelbard was dogsled, so most were making a final trip. Two days in Tromok and then back to Grimsbal for the worst of the winter.

As Calon Gan stood on the deck watching the harbour of Grimsbal recede into the distance and shivering slightly, one of the traders spoke to him.

"Not seen you on this trip before," he commented.

"I have not been to Skrelbard for many years."

"Nothing much seems to change there. I've been trading with them for fifteen years. Take Tromok, it's their only trading port,but it's a small harbour, all little buildings. I've seen much less important places down south look better."

"The Skrel do live simply."

"Not a life for me. They're nice people though. I have a bit of property in Alghol, nice house for the wife and kids. Let's people know I'm doing well."

Fortunately, he did not ask what took Gan to Skrelbard and the older man soon made the excuse of being cold and headed for his cabin. Like the others it was extremely small and most passengers preferred to spend time in the main room where they ate. Grok and Kalt were there talking. Another of the traders appeared to be engrossed in accounts at one end of the table.

Grok glanced at Gan as he passed by and returned his attention to Kalt who had also been abroad making investigations.

"There are hints," said Kalt.

"If we are lucky, they are just rumours. But they could be acting cautiously," Grok replied.

"That would make the situation more dangerous. We must know if they were recruiting. What does that old man want in Skrelbard?"

"I don't know. He's one of the Freidyn, so maybe they are worried as well. We happened to meet near Alghol and he asked if he could travel with me."

"Do you trust him?"

"The Freidyn were with us against the Council last time, so yes, for now. He may well be more dangerous than he looks though."

Chapter III

The temperature fell as the ship continued its journey north. The mountain peaks of Skrelbard were just visible as the sun set on the fourth day. The following morning saw the ship arriving at Tromok's harbour. As the trader had said, it did not look like a major port. The bay it sat on was sizeable but the area of the docks in their natural harbour was small. The city sat huddled under its surrounding mountains and covered with snow.

More snow was blowing around as the passengers disembarked and Grok said goodbye to Kalt. He turned his attention to Calon Gan.

"Do you know where you are going?"

"I was told merely to look around. I have no plans."

"The Skrelgrun Inn will be the best place to stay. Lok will not charge you."

Picking up Calon Gan's baggage as well as his backpack, the Skrel set off. Wondering why the innkeeper would not charge him, Calon Gan followed. Grok led the way through the streets with the assurance of a skrel who knew his way around, occasionally speaking to passers by who he knew. There were a number of humans and barances around but no elves. Calon Gan mentioned it to Grok, who laughed.

"The elves see themselves as the peak of culture, art and general civilization. They rank us with the wolves and badgers. If they came here, they could not keep believing that."

Elves tended to be tolerant of humans, but less so of other races. They had the most rigid class system of any society and considered art to be the highest of all achievements. Lower class elves did the work to feed and clothe the higher classes, following the strict instructions of higher ranked elves. The elves that travelled were of the higher classes and thus regarded themselves as a cut above just about everyone they met.

After about ten minutes of walking, they reached the Skrelgrun Inn. The main room was quiet as they walked in and an older skrel was wiping the bar.

Grok spoke."Lok!"

The Skrel looked up. "Grok y Gremnor! Tola! Come quickly!"

He hurried around from behind the bar and clapped Grok on the shoulder.

"How are you?"

"Doing well."

Tola made her entrance from the back regions, with a reaction similar to Lok's. She hugged Grok, her head barely reaching his chest.

"This is Calon Gan of the Freidyn," rumbled Grok as he disengaged Tola.

"Good morning, sir," said Lok. "I hope our rooms will be comfortable for you. "

"I am sure they will be. It has been many years since I have been in Skrelbard. The hospitality is something I have long remembered and measured others by."

"I must make you lunch," said Tola, bustling off to the kitchen.

"I have a task to do first. I will not be long," growled Grok, easing his pack to the floor.

Lok steered Calon Gan into the private parlour as Grok left the inn. "It will be more comfortable in here. Can I get you something to drink?"

"A hot cup of *cwr* will be most welcome. Thank you."

Lok followed Tola into the kitchen, then returned to the fire where Calon Gan was sitting.

"Have you known Grok long?"

"Not long. We met by chance and he agreed to be my companion for this journey. He is an exceptional Skrel."

"He is."

"You know him well?"

"He was...wed to our second daughter."

Calon Gan looked at Lok inquiringly, "Was?"

"Most people, I would say, 'He will tell you sometime.' Not Grok. I will tell you quickly before Tola returns." He paused. "Our daughter, Aula, was killed by humans. Part of a group called Pure Land."

"I know of them and I despise them."

"Others were killed in the attack including our grandson Krarg and Aula's unborn baby. Grok and others were away from Tolgath when the attack happened. They learned of it when they returned home and caught the humans before they could leave the island. Then Grok went alone to face Death."

"To face Death?"

"He used Yn Telkat an Relkat to call Death to him."

"Yn Telkat an Relkat?"

"An ancient Skrel rite, rarely used. The legend is

that Gralk al Gron was responsible. He was leader of a skrel tribe attacked by elves claiming they had been given part of the land of Skrelbard. Most of the tribe were killed, yet Gralk and his mages refused to kill the elves. They used other means together with the winter to drive them away. No elf died though many were sickened and frostbitten. Death had been prepared to deal with a massacre. When he was not needed he gave Gralk the summoning ritual. He told Gralk that most beings would have killed the invaders and called him by their actions. The skrel tribe did not and so Death would allow them to call him another way. He gave no reason for doing so but it is believed that he allowed them to save life as they had been slow to take it. Death can see a short way into the future and told Gralk that he and all skrel could call him if the situation was serious, aware that most beings will keep as far from Death as possible.

"Grok used the ritual and fought Death toe-to-toe but he could not get Aula and Krarg back. They had gone too far. But in his defeat Death allowed Grok to save one mortal, if he can call Death before the mortal is claimed. We know of no one else who has defeated Death though many have tried in their way." He paused. "Grok never told us about Death, we heard from a friend of his. Brelca had followed Grok to keep him safe and saw what happened. Some time later he told us the story to try and help. We grieved for our daughter, but Grok fought Death for her. He has no family so we became his family."

"Grok has no family?" Calon Gan asked.

"None that he knows of. His parents were killed in

the Great Storm five winters ago and his brother disappeared at sea the summer before."

"I did not know."

"Grok would not tell you himself. We lost our daughter and our grandson but we could not abandon our son-in-law easily. We take care of him when he passes through Tromok because we choose to."

He made an effort to brighten up as Tola entered with a pot full of *cwr*. After the drinks had been poured Gan asked a question.

"Why do you call Grok *'y Gremnor'*?"

"Because he is a wanderer," Tola answered. "Always has been according to the people in Tolgath."

The wanderer was at that point walking purposefully to a smithy on the edge of town. The blacksmith came outside as he approached and walked to meet him.

"Grok, you have returned to us."

"Did you think I would not, Friy?"

"Do you have it?"

Grok searched through his many pockets and produced the Stone of Erypmon. This hooded cloak and the coat he wore in summer had been made by Aula. Well aware of her husband's habit of filling his pockets with various items, she had added as many pockets as possible. His friends suspected she had done it as a joke but Grok appreciated them

"Good. Then we can destroy it," said Friy.

He walked back into the building followed by Grok. Once inside, he selected a large hammer with cloth wrapped around the head. Grok threw the stone into the fire and waited as Friy unwrapped the hammer. When the cloth was removed it revealed the engraved ideograms on the hammer.

"These were engraved exactly as your grandfather and Tharn instructed," Friy said. "They form a spell which will counter all the protections the Stone has and allow us to destroy it. It was not designed for an evil purpose so it has less protection."

The Stone was beginning to glow in the heat from the fire. Friy pulled it out and set it carefully on his anvil. Taking aim, he brought the hammer down on the stone. It disintegrated into a cloud of powder as an eerie scream emanated from it.

"That will slow them down," said Friy, with satisfaction.

"It will not stop them."

"There will always be those taken in by their promises and willing to help them."

"I will be heading to Tolgath tomorrow. We may meet again soon, though."

Calon Gan was still talking with Lok and Tola when Grok returned. Tola immediately poured him a mug of *cwr*. "I'm not convinced that you eat well when you're travelling," she fussed. "Now stay by the fire the while I make lunch."

Grok smiled as she left, with the indulgent expression males reserve for elderly female relatives.

"Are you travelling again?" asked Lok.

"Only to Tolgath. Unless I am needed somewhere."

"Kris is in town. I met him yesterday."

"How is he?"

"He is well. He takes the dogs back to Tolgath soon. You should be able to travel together."

Calon Gan asked a few questions of his host as they waited for the meal to arrive. The skrel innkeeper was talkative, with Grok occasionally making a comment. Then Tola appeared with many platters of food. Bread, sliced meats and cooked root vegetables. From outside the parlour came the noise of customers in the inn.

After eating some of the food, Lok left to tend the bar and Tola occasionally walked in to ensure the platters were being cleared.

Once they had eaten, neither Grok nor Calon Gan felt like moving for some time.

"Tola is known for her cooking," Grok said.

"That was an excellent meal," Calon Gan observed.

"After eating here, everyone needs to rest for a while."

Calon Gan had slipped into a light doze when Grok got up and stretched.

"Are you leaving?" the old man asked.

"I have things to do."

"Do you mind if I join you? I should like to see more of Tromok."

"I can guide you."

"You will be back later?" Lok asked, as he saw them leaving.

"Yes, we wil not be long," Grok replied.

"I will take your bags up to your rooms."

Grok and Calon Gan left the inn and walked along the street. The clouds were gathering overhead, giving the town a gloomy look.

Grok bought some provisions that had just arrived on the boat they had used. Then he escorted Calon Gan around the town, showing the old man some of the buildings and the harbour. Occasionally, Grok would call into a store or someone's house for a brief conversation. Lastly, they went to a large open area containing several dog yards. Each dog was chained to a small kennel filled with straw. They barked excitedly as their visitors crossed to where a skrel had stopped working and turned to see who the dogs were barking at.

"Hey Kris! Hello, Grolon!" Grok added, as a dog leaped up and started licking him.

"Grok! How was the journey?"

"Went well. I got in this morning. Had lunch at the Skrelgrun."

"You can move already? Tola is slipping."

They both laughed and Grok introduced Calon Gan. "You heading back to Tolgath?" he added.

"The day after tomorrow. Just the one team."

"You have room for a passenger, Kris?"

"I do."

"Hmm." He turned to Gan, "Do you want to travel to Tolgath?"

"Yes, certainly."

"Good. Kris will take you in the sled. I will leave tomorrow on foot."

"There will be food ready for us then," Kris laughed.

Grok took the long route back to the inn to enable Calon Gan to see more of Tromok. When they reached the Skrelgrun again, Calon Gan decided to lie down for a while. Grok crossed to the window in his own room and looked out, the snow the clouds had promised was starting to fall.

He was looking forward to spending some time in Tolgath, but he knew that with the spring he would want to travel again. He wondered if Aula would have coped with this kind of life and then pushed the thought away. Lighting a lamp, he began to organise his pack and set aside the warm clothing he would need for the journey to Tolgath.

Later that evening, Tola made another large meal and the travellers ate with Kris. Though snow was falling outside, the inn was warm and busy. Calon Gan moved around talking to various skrel. Later still, after Kris had left and Calon Gan had retired to his room , Grok drank beer as he talked to Dalk.

"I hear from Friy that the Stone is no more," Dalk said.

"It has been destroyed," Grok confirmed.

"If only that were the end of it. Is there a way to stop them entirely?"

"None that I know of."

"I once heard that those three artefacts were chosen because they gave the best results. It is possible that the Stone could be replaced with another similar artefact."

"Where did you hear of that?" Grok asked, concerned.

"I was talking to a Corbusian scholar. He had read of the Council working with magical items to discover which would achieve their aims."

"Are there any records of what they discovered?"

"No. It is thought that they have all been lost."

"Good. There have been some stories out of Grimevil that worry me."

"If the Council should reform and find the other artefacts then we are all in danger," said Dalk, draining his tankard. "I should leave now while I can still stand."

"*Na dur*, Dalk."

A short time after that, Lok started moving his customers out of the door as the hour of the inn's closing approached.

It was some time later that he returned to the bar, having heard noises there. The dying fire illuminated a large figure by the window.

"Go back to bed. I could not sleep." said Grok's voice. He lifted a mug. "Mulled wine. The coin is on the bar."

"*Na dur,* Grok."

"*Na dur.*"

As the innkeeper left, Grok sighed and drank some wine. The thoughts of Aula and Krarg had kept returning in the dark. He supposed that if he still had them he would be willing to defend Skrelbard if needed, but he would not be actively trying to stop the enemy. He could see his life heading in two directions dependent on defeating those who would follow in the footsteps of the Council of Barakelth. Failure, death and destruction. Success, more wandering and what?

For the first time in many months he thought of Brelca. The last time they met had been stormy. Brelca couldn't understand why Grok wanted to travel away from Skrelbard. Grok couldn't understand Brelca's inability to accept his wanderlust. The next time he returned to Tolgath, Brelca was dead. Killed while defending the village from a demon attack. Maybe if he had tried harder to get Brelca to travel, his friend would still be alive.

The snow was still falling. A flake for each regret in the world, as the saying went. Grok continued to sit and watch the flakes fall.

Chapter IV

He left Tromok early the next day. Lok and Tola made sure that he had more than enough food for the journey. His road led to the north of the town, he followed the main trail for some time before branching off. The main trail led through the Pass of Kergol, Grok was taking the lesser used Pass of Gronman, which was narrower and higher but the route was shorter.

The trail began to steepen, Grok was equal to it, though with the fresh snow it was heavy going. He paused briefly to eat and drink before going on, his aim was to be at the pass near nightfall.

The light was failing by the time he reached the pass. He turned round at looked back at Tromok, parts of the city were hidden by the foothills but he could just make it out, the last rays of the setting sun gave it a reddish hue reflected by some bonfires burning. It was a peaceable scene. He turned and walked through the pass. A short distance beyond the pass, on the other side of the mountains, was an area often used by travellers as a campsite. It was protected by the mountains from much of the weather and there would often be wood for a fire. There were evergreens around the site, like travellers , they were protected by the mountains and grew well.

Darkness had come by the time he reached the site, but like all skrel his night vision was excellent. He made a small fire and set some snow to melt. Most of his provisions could be eaten cold but he made *cwr* for warmth. As he sat by his fire and ate supper, the moon rose. Grok cut some boughs from the nearby trees and placed them by the fire as a base for his bed. After checking his fire would last the night, he wrapped himself in his cloak and a blanket and lay down on his improvised bed.

He was awake before the dawn, the temperature didn't encourage lie ins. After breakfast, he doused the fire and set off. The trail led into a valley that itself was well above Tromok before climbing again. When the sun had reached its highest point he stopped to eat before continuing. The trail led through the forest as it left the higher mountains and Grok looked for tracks as he went along. The usual animals had been around since the last snowfall, but no skrel. A wolf followed him at a distance for some time, Grok enjoyed the company. The wolves of Skrelbard were never hunted and were curious about the skrel. Grok always attracted wolves and dogs. He liked them but had never understood why they liked him so much.

The Klornac River had not frozen entirely, so he used the boulders that had been placed on the riverbed to cross the only major obstacle on his route.

Darkness had fallen once again as the trail skirted a another hill and led into Tolgath. A strong northerly wind had begun to blow, so the streets were empty. Grok walked past the longhouse and paused to consider whether to go in and see if Zen was there. Though Dak might be as well, so he continued on.

Just before the edge of the village he reached a small log building set against the hillside. He opened the door and picked up a candle just inside on a small ledge. He set his pack on the floor and, after closing the door, began to make a fire in the central fireplace. The house began to warm as he lit a lamp and sat in one of the simple chairs. At last, he was home.

Chapter V

The house was pleasantly warm and supper was cooking. The furniture was simple but comfortable. Apart from some old manuscripts lying around, the only decoration was an old sword on one wall. Hanging below the sword was a bow and a quiver of arrows, both showing signs of much use. A large battleaxe was propped against one wall near a stone archway leading into a natural cave, which formed two bedrooms and a larder.

Knowing how fast news travelled around Tolgath, Grok wasn't surprised when he had a visitor after supper. He was drinking *cwr* and poured a mug for his guest.

"It is good to see you again, Grok."

"I have not been back long, Tharn."

"Have you seen much?"

"A lot and a little. Depending on what you want to know."

When Grok wasn't being silent he was often obscure.

"Now you are back, Zen wants to see you. Tomorrow."

"How is he?"

"The same as usual. Is there news of danger?"

"He told you?"

"Yes."

"Nothing definite and the Stone is destroyed. I suspect there is a storm coming in the south. We need to be ready."

"Zen told me of last time. It could happen again?"

"Very little has changed. There are still those who want power."

The following morning he called in to see Brelca's mother, Pola. She had an encyclopaedic knowledge of the healing plants of Skrelbard and was a healer of skill.

"Grok! Welcome back."

"How are you?"

"I am well. A mother will miss a child for all her life, it disturbs me that you are still affected by his death." Whatever you mentioned to one Skrel in Tolgath, was passed around to those also interested.

"I tried to persuade him to travel with me not long before. I should have done more."

"You could not see what would happen if he stayed. He could not understand what drove you. Neither of you was at fault. He died saving others, I take what comfort I can from that." She paused and looked away for a moment. "Is there news from over the Morleyd?"

"Some. There are skirmishes to the south as the lords argue about land. Some call for the rulers to have more power, but others remember when that happened in the past and many of their people died at the hands of tyrants. There is trouble ahead."

On the trail between Tromok and Tolgath, Kris and Calon Gan had stopped to rest the dogs and eat.

"I still do not know why you are here," said Kris.

"I am not certain myself. Long ago, the Freidyn looked into the future. It appears that your race is the key to coming events. Death and destruction or peace and life. We know that you can choose your path and so choose what happens to the rest of the world. Yet we do not know what choice will lead to which future."

"You should talk to Zen. He will be in Tolgath. But be careful if you talk to him and Grok together. Either they'll be clear or Grok won't say anything and Zen will be cryptic. They seem to understand each other though."

"About Grok."

"If you want to know anything about him, ask anyone but Grok."

"Who is he?"

"A wanderer, a hunter, a carver. One who can survive alone. A warrior and a *korloth*."

"A what?"

"There is no word for it in your language. When he travels he learns things. He tells them to others who it might help. He is direct if you are, unlike Zen. He trusts and so is never betrayed. Though if he is mistaken about someone, he can be their worst enemy."

Back in Tolgath, Grok walked into the Longhouse. An old skrel was sitting by the central fire with two cups of *cwr*.

"Grok y Gremnor," the old skrel said.

"Zen," Grok replied.

Grok accepted the proffered mug and they sat in silence for some time.

"You saw Pola."

Grok nodded.

"She is correct."

Grok raised his eyebrows.

"Wisdom is not given, but gathered."

Grok continued looking into his mug.

"When one has gathered enough to know that regrets of the past poison the present, it is but a short time before that present ends."

"What of the future?"

"There is but a kernel of truth in the husks of falsehoods that make up the future. Too often it is recognised only when the future is past."

Grok did not respond.

"Any Fate which tried to direct your path would

fail, most likely due to receiving a battleaxe to the head." He paused. "Too many of the Skrelton are old. To those like you will our world be entrusted."

"There is another."

"Thenk."

Grok looked at Zen from under his brows. "No, a werewolf," He was silent for a moment. "Where is Thenk?"

"His absence from Tolgath is all that I can state."

Grok returned his gaze to the *cwr*.

"What have you seen to the south?"

"There is much happening. I found the Stone of Erypmon in Tildeth and it is destroyed. A Freidyn helped me in Corbus and another is travelling here with Kris. The lords to the south are arguing and fighting about land. The people do not care unless they are forced to fight."

"A Freidyn helped you?"

"Someone knew what I was doing, I think. Dence helped when they attacked."

Zen was silent for a while considering matters.

"You should begin the hunt."

Grok drained his mug and left the Longhouse. As he did so, a figure emerged from the shadowed corner in which he had been lurking.

"You are not pleased," said Zen, still looking at the fire.

The figure joined him, but remained standing. "Wherever he goes, trouble finds him."

"You are old, Dak. With age comes fear."

"Comes wisdom."

"The true path to wisdom involves recognising the

fear for what it is."

"Grok called Death to us."

"As others did years before for similar reasons. It was to fight him for Aula and Krarg, as well as the young one. How many of us would do that? Grok may never be a leader, but he will achieve much."

Some hours later, Kris and Calon Gan arrived in Tolgath. They saw Grok on the street talking to Pola, he handed her the deerskins he was holding and walked to Kris' dogs.

"Hey dogs!" he said as they jumped up to greet him. "We have deer for supper," he told the others.

"Sounds good," said Kris. "I will be there later."

Calon Gan left Kris to take care of his dogs and joined Grok as he walked home. On the way, Grok told him that Zen wanted to meet him and would call by later. It was after they had eaten supper that Zen arrived, Grok and Kris were drinking beer that Lok had sent up. Calon Gan was sipping at a mug of *cwr*.

"Good evening," said Zen, walking in.

"Zen! *Cwr*?"

"Thank you, Grok. Calon Gan, it is you I have come to see. We have things to talk of and it is not a tale that Grok will share."

"You know me too well."

"You know a little of our history? Our battle against the creatures from the Outer Darkness?"

"A version I suspect. I have heard many different tales from different lands. Most of which have a hero from the teller's land."

The skrel smiled.

"As history fades, we should expect that. Like your order, we pass along the true accounts. There were no Wars of the Gods as the Caran Church and their ilk claim. These creatures, the Xetal as they are known to us, appear to have come from somewhere away from our world. Perhaps somewhere close to the region of the demons who break through occasionally. The Xetal were able to take control of humans, elves and barances, to invade them. For some reason the skrel were not affected. We led an attack against them and they were banished to where they came from. The early members of the Freidyn were there, as were many others."

"The texts tell of such a battle and of the skrel's part," Calon Gan interjected.

"Ever since we have kept watch. We know the Utahns believe that the Xetal were sent to rid the world of evil, they are small in numbers and have little power. There have been groups forming and disbanding since the war. As with the Caran Church, they see evil everywhere except in themselves. They are not our concern. The Stone of Erypmon has been destroyed, but there are other ways to contact the Darknesses. That is what we call the realms of the demons. Those who live in the Darkness can come through of their own volition, and do so. Those of the Outer Darkness must be called and are far more dangerous. There will always be some who believe the sweet lies of those who call the Xetal. The Council of Barakelth has faded, but it could be revived. We must be prepared for the worst. The Stone was but one part of the ritual used by the Council. The

Hammer of Colwen and the Spear of Pyra were also used. Their whereabouts are unknown."

"The Freidyn once looked into the future. They foresaw two futures. The skrel were important in the choice; that is why I am here."

"So it begins," whispered Zen. "There are no signs of the Council reforming, but there are many whispers. Grok, we will need Thenk."

"I will look for Leku as well."

"Are you sure?" Zen asked. Grok trusted Leku implicitly, yet other skrel were far more wary of him.

Grok turned his head to look directly at the old skrel.

"You are. Very well," Zen said as he prepared to leave. "I will see you at the Longhouse tomorrow for the Skrelton. Dak will be there, Grok. Do not mention Leku. *Na dur.*"

"Who is Leku?"asked Calon Gan when Zen had left.

"A friend," growled Grok.

Chapter VI

Grok and Calon Gan were at the Longhouse early. Zen was already there and formally invited them to the Skrelton meeting. Grok poured a mug of *cwr* and looked at the various skrel coming in. Dak arrived early, as he always did. Lauk and Dorl were with him, Grok sighed mentally. Dak was no doubt trying to turn them to his way of thinking. Although a skrel of high intelligence, he was the worst kind of traditionalist. He would oppose any new idea simply because it was not the way things had always been done. One of the curses of old age was the rigidity of mind that came to some.

Then there was Rana. Similar to Dak but her dislike was much more focused, specifically against Grok. As far as Grok could tell, he annoyed her merely by existing. She would side with Dak. He saw her mouth tighten as she noticed him sitting near the wall. He had decided to follow Zen's advice and not mention Leku. Zen knew how to deal with protocol and formality, Grok was happy without either.

Pola and Coni arrived. Pola was the youngest of the Skrelton, she would agree with Zen, he was sure. Coni, maybe. The famed skrel Rowan al Brwss had said, "To let all have a say in the decisions of Skrelbard is not the best way to work. But it is better than anything else we have thought of." His thoughts were interrupted by Calon Gan.

"What is the Skrelton?" the old man asked.

"They are the leaders of Tolgath. Every settlement has a Skrelton and each Skrelton has a member of the Skrelton in Svaltok."

"The Skrelton in Svaltok is the one that speaks for Skrelbard?"

"Yes. Each member is honour bound to support the view of their home Skrelton. Most of the Skrelton are old. Some have wisdom, but all are able to be spared from other duties."

"How do you choose the Skrelton?"

"When a member dies, any skrel who has seen at least fifteen winters can propose a new member. Any of us can then refuse to allow that member a place.

We know that Tolgath has skrel of many opinions and we make sure that the Skrelton has many opinions. I may not like what Dak and Rana say, but they must be allowed to say it."

With the Skrelton present, Zen stood up and began to speak.

"You may know of the stories that have come out of Tildeth and Grimevil. Those on the high borders of Tildeth have seen dark works being carried out in Grimevil. More demons have been seen within the mountains. The Lonskat of Grimevil is known to have studied dark magics and now that he is the supreme leader we must be concerned that he will try to use them against any he considers an enemy. It seems that he is a descendant of those who promised Grimevil's support to the Council in years past. He may well choose to continue a family tradition. Grok y Gremnor and Friy y Relddu have destroyed the Stone of Erypmon. But that may not stop those who wish to call the Xetal. We have one of the Freidyn with us. It seems as though a crisis is coming soon. We must decide what to do."

"Nothing," said Dak. "We are safe here in Skrelbard."

Grok growled menacingly, causing Zen to look over at him. "That is not an option," said the old skrel. "Calon Gan, if you will."

Calon Gan stood and addressed the Skrelton. "Many, many years ago my Order looked into the future and recorded what they observed. Soon we will reach the limit of those observations. For our near future they saw two different scenes. In one the skrel stayed on Skrelbard, there was death and destruction here and all over the known lands. The other they observed was one in which skrel had left this island to fight against those who would betray our world to the Xetal. There was no major destruction and they could see very little change from what is our present."

"Thank you," said Zen, as Calon Gan sat down next to Grok. "We know that as of one month ago the Council had not reformed. There were no signs of immediate concern. But that merely indicates that we have time to prepare if we wish to avoid the destruction foreseen by the Freidyn.

"I suggest that we propose to the Skrelton in Svaltok that we prepare for another battle with the Xetal and the Council of Barakelth, that we send some of our people to stop their plans before they can fully begin. I will now ask each of you to speak."

Dak stood up. "All we have heard are rumours. There is no need to do anything. If it should be necessary, then Skrelbard can act alone and immediately." He pointed to Grok. "Why should we act on the word of a warrior who cannot walk and think? Grok always brings trouble. This is the skrel who has fought against members of this Skrelton in defence of a werewolf! I am not going to move for his expulsion from Tolgath, I know it is not worth my breath. When we know of trouble, we will so act. We have always waited for knowledge. We will do so again."

"He only sees me as a warrior," Grok whispered. "Therefore, I cannot be anything else."

As Dak sat down, Pola stood up. "You know what happened to my son, Brelca. The demon attacks will be nothing compared to what will happen if the Xetal are unleashed. By the time we have proof here in Skrelbard, we may have lost Grimevil. The Council may be reforming now. We cannot know but we can prepare. Brelca died to save Tolgath. If we do nothing now then his sacrifice will have been for nothing." She sat down.

Lauk stood up next. "I had been minded to argue for doing nothing, but what Calon Gan has told us has changed my mind. I know of the Freidyn. If they are worried, then we should act."

Rana stood up.

"Here we go," muttered Grok.

"On the word of a wandering warrior, we are willing to wage war? May I remind you that this is the only Skrel in a hundred years to use Yn Telkat an Relkat. As Dak has stated, he always brings trouble. Now he wants us to travel and fight against an enemy that does not exist. The Stone is destroyed, the Council is no more. The Freidyn themselves do not know what to make of the future, they cannot tell when our people leave Skrelbard to fight. If the Xetal attack, then we act. Only then. That is the way we have always done things. Further, I move that the friend of werewolves leave this assembly."

"Grok is here at my invitation," Zen said. "Only I can tell him to leave. That is the way things have always been done."

It was Coni's turn. "We are not arguing about waging war. We are talking about preparing for a war that will almost certainly occur, unless those who would call the Xetal are stopped. Knowledge is needed. If that comes from sending Skrel out to investigate with the ability to fight, then that is what we must do. Grok has proved himself to be a warrior who is intelligent. He has nothing to lose. He will fight for Skrelbard, not just for his family."

Dorl spoke. "The Xetal never invaded Skrelbard during the war. We are safe here. If we are asked for help then we may give it. If the Xetal sue for peace, we may give it. We do not need anyone else. We should do nothing."

"Very well," said Zen. "I call the vote. Do we prepare for an invasion by the Xetal and attempt to prevent it?"

Dak, Rana and Dorl voted, no. Pola, Lauk and Coni, yes.

"My vote is yes," said Zen. "We will send our decision to Svaltok. If any of you see Sket, please tell him that he is needed."

The group broke up.

"What happens now?" Calon Gan asked Grok.

"Zen will write the decision. Sket will take it to the Skrelton at Svaltok There, they will decide what Skrelbard will do."

"You will do what they say?"

"Maybe." He stood up. "I am going to look for Leku and Thenk. I will not be back till after dark. Do not leave Tolgath."

He left the Longhouse, Calon Gan watched him go. Pola came over carrying two mugs of cwr, she handed one to the old man.

"So, Grok is looking for Thenk?"

"Thank you. Yes, he is."

"You will help us?"

"As far as I can. There are not many of the Freidyn left. I may well be needed elsewhere in the future, but it will be to the same end."

"If you can, take care of Grok."

"He is important to you?"

"Grok and my son were once close friends. Brelca could not understand Grok's wanderlust. Even after Aula and Krarg were killed. Eventually, it ended their friendship. Brelca was always the one to get out of situations by talking, while Grok was never diplomatic. He has not changed. When he is around it reminds me of happier times, I do not want to lose any more of our young skrel."

Chapter VII

Grok's boots broke the silence of the forest as he crunched through the snow, another week and he would need snowshoes. He was an hour's walk out of Tolgath; Leku would be somewhere nearby. The werewolf had a few huts and caves here and there that he moved between as the mood took him. He disliked staying in one place for any length of time. The general reaction of non-werewolves had made him cautious of making his presence obvious.

Grok scanned the area for sign, there was none so far. One of the huts was just ahead, but Leku was not there either. He paused to consider. It could take a long time to track down Leku and return to Tolgath., there was an easier way. Grok took a deep breath and howled, the noise echoed around the mountains.

He sat on a log to wait and eat. The sun had travelled past three tall trees when he heard a twig break to his left. "Hey, Leku."

From his left a voice complained, "How am I supposed to sneak up if you call out like that?"

Grok laughed. The werewolf emerged from the trees and stood looking at Grok. He leapt across the gap between them and grasped Grok's forearms in the Skrel handshake. Grok's hands squeezed the muscles of Leku's forearms and so, according to tradition, they had demonstrated that neither held a weapon.

"It has been a long time," Leku said. "Come inside." He walked into the hut. Grok followed him in and rested his bow against a wall.

Leku sniffed the air. "By the scents, you were at the Longhouse earlier and Tromok a couple of days ago. You walked to Tolgath and you have been on a boat recently. What has been happening?"

"We destroyed the Stone of Erypmon. A few of us have been travelling. It looks like the Xetal will return. The Council have not reformed. Yet, I have heard some stories out of Grimevil that would make your fur curl."

"Things are bad?"

"Not yet, but they will be. The barriers are weakening." He reached into one of his many pockets and pulled out a long curved claw. Leku took it and sniffed it.

"When did you get this?"

"Three weeks ago, when I killed the demon that bore it."

Leku gave it back. "This is bad."

"If the Council reforms, it will be worse."

"What help do you need?"

"I do not know yet. We need to find Thenk. The Skrelton has voted to prepare for trouble. We cannot wait for the Xetal to reach the Morleyd. Some of us must head south."

"*Y Gremnor* speaks. You have an idea?"

"A desperate one. To take on the Council directly before they can do anything."

"You should see if your grandfather knew of anything that could help us against the Council. He discovered much about the Xetal and the Council that none of us knows."

"Hmm. Have you seen Thenk?"

"He is nearby training some of the young hunters and woodskrel. Trying to train them. One of the woodskrel was nearly hit by a tree he was felling." He sighed. "They fear me and they have respect for the wild animals they hunt. They forget that plants are alive and can be as dangerous as *brants*. I will send Thenk to Tolgath."

"Thanks. Are he and Elea still not thinking of marriage?"

"Yes," Leku chuckled. "Everyone in the village thinks they are a match except them."

"Tolfast begins tomorrow. I am the host of the Eenfast. You are welcome."

"Maybe."

"I should go. I will see you soon."

"Grok, there may be deaths if we do this. Do not prevent Death from taking me."

Grok looked at him for a moment. "I will not."

Chapter VIII

Far from Skrelbard were two figures, dressed in red robes. They stood together on a windswept hilltop with only a few uninterested sheep for company. They had merely nodded to each other as they met, each expecting the other to be there. They stood in silence as they watched the sun near the horizon. As its last rays were hidden by the land the taller of the two raised his arms and spoke, "*Elcon renda un pace.*"

"*Un pace deteum parla,*" the other replied.

"It is done. We will recruit more, but here it begins. The Council of Barakelth exists once more!"

"After all the years of planning, we now approach our goal."

"Yes, Chene. We approach but are still far, with many impediments on our journey." He turned to look at the elf, she was gazing at the mountains where the sun had set with a determined look in her pale grey eyes.

"We will overcome those impediments, be they of land, magic or Skrel," she said. "When the Council of Barakelth has recruited the one hundred, none shall stand against us. You will be the undisputed leader of the known lands, Geoe."

Her human companion nodded. "There is much we must do to gain the one hundred. Tonb will meet us tomorrow and he will bring more with him. Then we must go out and spread the word to those who would support us. We must stay silent to those who we know would oppose our plans for the peace of the world. We are still few in number, as such we are weak when pitted against our enemies. They will learn of the true glories the Council has when we are powerful. Until that time comes we must hide ourselves from their gaze."

"I have heard of skrel leaving their island to travel in fairer lands."

"They sully those lands with their presence. The skrel are not welcome in this Council, I do not welcome then into my land. Even the Xetal turned away in distaste from their monstrous presence."

He began to carefully walk down the hillside, motioning his companion to follow. "Remember Chene, our allies can not help us to form our new Council. We must do that to prepare for their arrival. Once they are here, we can begin to implement our plans for peace. Then, we take our revenge on those whose ancestors fought the Council on the Plains of Harabrum."

Chapter IX

Zen and Calon Gan were at the window of the Longhouse when Grok returned, with a deer over his shoulders and dragging a boar behind him. He carried them to one corner and piled them there.

"For tomorrow," he growled.

"Did you find those you sought?" Zen asked.

"Thenk will be here soon."

"Good. And the other? He will aid us?"

"Yes."

"Hmm."

"Zen has been telling me some of Skrel history," said Calon Gan. "It is most interesting."

"Hmm."

"Is something wrong?"

"I do not know, there is something. I will see you later." He left the building.

"There are many here who do not share Dak's opinion of Grok," said Zen. "Yet, they think of him as a simple skrel. I think it is because he does not show what goes on in his mind to most of us. He reminds me of his grandfather in some ways."

"He was a scholar?" Calon Gan asked, having seen Grok reading a manuscript the previous night.

"He was many things, including a scholar. He knew that our *larhwnens* only tell of Skrel history and so he wrote much and taught his children and grandchildren to read. He also had dealings with the Freidyn of Alghol and gave them some of his work."

"He was Gron ar Tolgath? My order still holds him in high regard."

"Yes, Grok is Gron's grandson."

Later that night Grok stood outside his house. In spite of the cold, he was bare-chested and holding something that hung on a cord round his neck. Calon Gan came out behind him, wrapped in a fur.

"Grok, I heard a yell."

"Just a bad dream." He gently pushed the old man back inside and closed the door. "Go back to bed."

Grok settled into a chair by the fire as Calon Gan lingered at the archway, looking back at him.

"I will be well," Grok told him, correctly reading the expression on the old man's face. Calon Gan nodded and returned to his bed.

Grok reached for a flask of mead and poured some out into a wooden mug. He put the dream down to anxiety. It had been in a forest where he had been ambushed by a demon, something that had happened in the past. He had attacked the demon with his axe.

The demon fought back furiously but Grok was able to kill it. When it fell to the ground, it turned into Aula as he had last seen her. There was a sound in the bushes. As he turned, he saw the scared face of Krarg, just before the child ran. That was when he cried out and awoke.

He knew that Krarg and Aula were gone forever. Gron, assuming the baby was male, was also gone.

He swallowed the mead in one go and set the mug down. He had not been able to save his family. The least he could do now was try to save the world.

He was still in a thoughtful mood twelve hours later as he set up the deer and the boar for roasting. Tolfast went on for three weeks with a number of feasts. Eenfast was the first. By custom, one male in the community was chosen at random as host; other feasts were either family affairs or would be communal with every family contributing food.

Calon Gan was looking through Gron's notes which

Grok had loaned to him. Most of the Skrel history was oral but some had been written. He had spent much time talking to the *larhwnens*, the wordweavers, on his previous visit and discovered that there was more to the skrel than he had realised. He was deep in thought when he heard a voice behind him. "Calon Gan?"

He turned to see a skrel standing there, as tall as Grok but with fair hair and a chip off the left lower fang.

"You may not recognise me. I am Thenk."

"Thenk. You were but a lad last time I saw you. I knew your father well."

"I do remember you. Though it was many years ago."

"I was sorry to hear of Krarg's death."

"An accident that could not have been prevented. Regrettably, I do not need to ask why you are here."

"You have heard the stories?"

"Yes, I have also travelled in the south. I have heard the decision of the Skrelton and approve of it. There are those who will wait until trouble is past the horizon and bearing down on them before they will act. This is a matter where we cannot wait so long. However, this is a time of celebration. We should forget our troubles for the time being."

"What is Tolfast?"

"Travel in Skrelbard can be difficult at this time and outside is even more so. Our ancestors were forced to spend time keeping warm in their villages instead of working and travelling. So they began to celebrate the fact that better weather was coming," explained Thenk.

After the sun had set all, the skrel of Tolgath began to fill the hall. There was roast boar, venison, poultry, vegetables and sweet puddings. It was traditional for the host to make a speech before the feast. Kris and Thenk had placed bets on how short it would be. Everyone was at the table ready to help themselves to food as Grok stood up.

"Enjoy yourselves. Eat!"

Thenk won the bet.

The feast started a period of relative calm for Gan and the skrel. While nothing was forbidden during Tolfast, the skrel disliked such laws, it was usual for skrel to relax.

Calon Gan offered to help with household chores, Grok refused, growling that it wasn't skrel culture. The old man spent most of his time talking to Zen and others to learn about the history of Skrelbard. Some, including Dak and Rana, discreetly avoided him.

"Guilt by association," explained Zen. "You came here at Grok's invitation, therefore you are aligned with him. There are some skrel who cannot tolerate views different from their own and so find themselves in conflict with our culture. Fortunately, they are a small minority and are not able to inflict their narrowness of mind on the rest of us. Though, we must tolerate them. The histories of the south show a form of government similar to ours has surfaced in many places, only to fall again. Often with the enthusiastic support of those affected."

"Skrelbard has never fallen to that?"

"No. Maybe because the Skrelton rules by

agreement, it cannot force its opinions. Travel between villages is not easy, especially in winter. A tyrant would not be able to control all skrel. As a race, we have no desire to rule or build grand monuments to ourselves which takes money. We have no army. All skrel are taught to ask questions."

"That is a good way to be."

"It has served us well for centuries." He sighed. "Grok does not make it easier on himself by being a friend of Leku. I sometimes think that if Aula and the children were still alive he would be more diplomatic about it. Now, he defends his friends as fiercely as his family."

Grok spent much of his time cutting wood and hunting. A week after Eenfast, Calon Gan met him outside the Longhouse. The skrel was looking at the clouds to the northeast.

"There is a big storm blowing in," he said, turning to look at Calon Gan. Once the snow starts go to my house, Zen's, Thenk's or Kris'. Do not stay in the Longhouse or go outside." With that he patted Gan's shoulder and hurried off.

The old man turned back into the Longhouse to look at more writings. Before long, the light had failed and he needed a lamp. He found an oil lamp sitting on a shelf. Using a flint, he managed to light the wick after a false start. Outside, the snow began to fall. He was intent on his reading when the door opened. Kris and Zen were there.

"Come, Calon Gan!" called Zen.

Gan remembered Grok's words, blew out the lamp, and joined them. Finding Grok's house empty, Zen took Calon Gan to his own small home. Kris escorted them before running through the snow back to his own house. The firepit in Zen's house held a warming blaze as they took off their warm coats. Smaller than Grok's house, it was tidier but still as utilitarian.

Calon Gan gazed out of the small window at the snow. Never before had he seen it come down with such ferocity. Zen joined him. "If Grok is still outside he will be safe," the old Skrel said. "No weather in the world would face Grok when he is angry."

A blizzard was developing as three large figures walked into Tolgath and towards Grok's house. Once inside, Thenk and Leku shook snow off themselves as Grok secured the door. The wind howled as they built up the fire to heat stew and *cwr*. Grok poured generous shots of mead for each of them to counteract the chill.

"No one need know you are here,Leku," said Thenk.

"If they do, they will keep quiet," growled Grok, flexing a fist.

Thenk grinned at him. "Ever the diplomat."

"Diplomacy is just fancy lies."

Leku paused to listen to the wind. "You were right. I should be here."

"We win!" shouted Thenk. "We told you this storm was one where you should be in Tolgath."

As the three friends applied themselves to stew, Calon Gan and Zen were seated near the fire. The skrel was reciting.

"So it was that Krarg y Keltor lead the skrel into the final battle against the Xetal. The fighting was fierce and many of all races fell before it was ended. At last,the Xetal were forced back through the portal into the realm from which they came, but the price was high. Many of the southern lands were ravaged by the demons that had come with the Xetal. Leaders were deposed and emperors put in their place. Skrelbard was not immune; the skrel were sorely tried by imps and demons that appeared. Eventually the powers of Selkanefen the mage were enough to end the attacks on all lands. The mage died shortly thereafter, exhausted by the effort. From that point on, the magic began to fade.

"Yet the land of Grimevil stayed for some time under a dark cloud where, fearful travellers whispered, unspeakable rites were practiced.

"Krarg insisted that the Skrel should not withdraw from the world and some should travel. They were to seek knowledge that would aid in future times. So it was that the skrel learned of the disappearance of the major artefacts that allowed the Council of Barakelth to contact the Outer Darkness. The Stone of Erypmon, the Hammer of Colwen and the Spear of Pyra vanished from the ken of the lands. The skrel knew then that the world was not safe."

He stopped speaking and drank water from a mug. "Ever since, through the long years, we have kept some of our people travelling and learning. I suppose, like the Freidyn, we are guarding the world."

"Not a position anyone would willingly accept, I fear, but one that someone must hold. Fair few in the southern lands know of the old days save in legend. Fewer would believe the Xetal could return."

"So, it becomes our responsibility to avoid another such war, if we can. We hope that no land will side with the Council, but power is desired by too many."

By the following afternoon the storm had passed, leaving much fresh snow covering Tolgath. Not only snow, Kris was at the edge of the village when he found a creature. It was not one the skrel were familiar with. Larger than any of the skrel, blue in colour, not furred and possessing long talons as well as four eyes set in the front of its head. Gan identified it as a *rakshinsa*. One kind of demon that had plagued the southern lands in times past. It had died from exposure to the storm.

The discovery was worrying to the skrel. It was a sign that the barriers were weakening. Grok, Calon Gan, Thenk and Zen debated what to do.

"We need to be aware of the dangers but there is a limit to what we four can do," said Zen.

"I would like to notify the Freidyn, but I fear that cannot happen," said Calon Gan.

"Not for some time," Grok told him.

"I will continue gathering information. The more knowledge I have, the better I can advise the Freidyn," Gan decided.

"There is no work tomorrow," said Zen. "It is the main day of Tolfast. We give gifts, eat and drink. We cook, but it is primarily a day to rest and enjoy ourselves."

"We must plan now so that when the spring comes we are ready," said Grok. "Even if the Council is at work, we cannot achieve anything until then."

Chapter X

Far to the south in Erein, the stranger Grok had seen in Grimsbal entered a remote inn. Snow swirled in with him and settled on the flagstones. He looked around and approached a man sitting by the fire. Without removing his hood, the stranger sat down and held out a piece of parchment. On it were words in an ancient language and a symbol, one Calon Gan would have recognised. The symbol of the Council of Barakelth. The man looked at it and his scarred face twisted into a smile.

"Who sent you?" he asked.

"Geoe."

"The man of red?"

"No, the man of white."

The scarred man nodded, the messenger was genuine. He accepted the parchment and placed it inside his leather jerkin. "*Elcon renda un pace,*" he said.

"*Un pace deteum parla,*" the other replied.

"Why does Geoe ask for me now?" the man asked, holding his hands to the fire.

His visitor's hood moved as the man looked around the inn. "He needs your help," he said, quietly. "There is someone who is not providing information needed by us."

"Return here at first light and take me to where Geoe is. I will assist him then."

The hooded stranger nodded and left the inn.

Geoe and Chene of the Council of Barakelth were in a remote house, in the land of Erein. The man from the inn had been admitted an hour earlier. He had spent the time since then in the cellar. The two Councillors sat in silence, though the screams from below had ceased earlier.

"What news, Tonb?" asked Geoe, as the cellar door opened and the man walked into the kitchen.

"He knew, but he was reluctant to talk," Tonb told them. "I persuaded him." He smiled and dabbed at a spot of blood on his jerkin.

"Where is the Hammer?"

"In the care of the DeHarl family of Maychel. They do not know what they have, they just keep it as instructed by an ancestor."

"We will relieve them of that burden. Tonb, you will ride with us," said Geoe.

"Thank you, I will return," Tonb said, as he prepared to leave.

"Do you know of the DeHarl family, Chene?" Geoe asked the elf.

"I do. There is a son of the house who may wish to help us," she told him. "He may allow us to find the Hammer without the help of Tonb."

"Maybe so. Though I would not like to deprive Tonb of his work. He takes so much joy in it."

"He does. I trust he has no magic abilities?"

"None at all, Chene."

"Good. Magic coupled to a mind such as that would even endanger this Council."

Chapter XI

The day dawned clear in Tolgath. Many of the inhabitants were out soon after calling in on friends, giving gifts and inviting to feasts.

Pola visited Grok's house to invite Calon Gan and Grok to dinner. "Thenk and Zen will also be coming," she told them.

"Thanks, " Grok replied. "We will come."

"If no one invites him he will probably not do anything," she confided to Calon Gan, as they stood in the doorway. "It is not a good day to be alone."

"What about Leku?" Calon Gan asked, after Pola had left.

"He told me he would be spending today alone."

The clouds threatened another storm as they gathered at Pola's house. Many skrel had passed through Grok's during the day and now, with the night advancing, was the time to group together.

First, the gifts were given. As Pola was hosting the gathering, she gave out hers first. Then the guests followed with their own gifts. Skrel would often make gifts to give to others and so Pola gave out cakes and clothing. Thenk had some dried meats and sticks. The sticks represented firewood that he would leave the following day. Calon Gan had little to give but the skrel waved away his apologies and accepted the gifts of spices and small items from the south that he had bought in Alghol. Zen gave them each small polished pieces of stone on which he had inked a likeness of each of them. Finally, Grok handed out some carvings he had made, gruffly remarking that they were not much. Calon Gan looked at his, a wolf running. The carving was delicate and the wolf looked almost alive. He thought of Grok carving such things for his ill-fated children and his vision misted.

The food was excellent, as was the company. For some time the Skrel and Calon Gan were able to forget about the threats from the south.

Thenk joined Calon Gan and Grok as they walked home in the falling snow. He muttered to the old man that he did not want Grok being alone that night. Calon Gan went to bed as soon as they arrived, feeling tired from the food and a long day. He held the carved wolf in his hand as he lay in bed, not wanting to be far away from it.

Thenk and Grok sat up by the fire, sipping mead in a companionable silence. Each was caught up in his own thoughts, Grok on Aula and the children, Thenk on his father and Grok.

"Why?" asked Grok after some time.

Thenk thought for a moment, he was used to Grok's short questions. "Dad told me to take care of you."

Grok raised an eyebrow.

"It is Tolfast. Everyone spends time with family or friends. It is not a good time to be alone. Also, I have known you so long, you could be dying of grief and never show it."

"Oh," Grok growled. He gave Thenk a long look, before he poured more mead and Thenk placed another log on the fire.

Chapter XII

A cold wind was blowing from the north as Calon Gan walked with Zen to the Longhouse. The *larhwnens* were performing that afternoon. When Grok had learned what their subject was to be he decided to go and see Leku for the day. As always in the winter, a large fire was burning in the Longhouse and it was warm. Zen set water to boil as other skrel began to walk in.

The *larhwnens* were the historians of Skrelbard. While bards would sing songs and tell fictions, the *larhwnens* would learn what had happened and pass along the truth. It was a point of honour with them to remember and transfer exactly what they were told to the following generations. While some skrel such as Gron had written down information they feared would be lost, most Skrel history was oral.

Zen prepared *cwr* as the building filled, listening to the *larhwnens* was popular, for skrel took their history seriously. A young skrel stood up.

"*Croesen,* friends! We have old and new history as we tell of the Stone Of Erypmon." The young *larhwnen* began the tale.

Erypmon was a mage from Gamelen who lived far in the past, a man noted for his appearance as much as for his magic. His single eye was sunken deeply into his head and half his nose was missing. He was, due to his appearance, unmarried, but of good character and reputation. Any of his neighbours could rely on him for help. Larger than many skrel, he was immensely strong and was famed for pulling a cart carrying a family from harm when their horse was lamed.

One day, his neighbour Allagrim, the son of Horgeil Redhair, came to him for aid. His lands and farmhands were being attacked by a vengeful ghost. Animals were hurt or vanishing and Telland Honisson had been killed by the ghost as he tended sheep.

Erypmon travelled with Allagrim to his house and stayed watchful through the night, looking for the ghost. Close to dawn, he saw it roaming near the house. Challenged by the mage, the ghost roared that it was the spirit of Brunor Tellson, continuing a feud that had ended with Brunor's death. The sun rose, the ghost vanished, and the mage returned to his home to think of a way to help Allagrim.

The ghost returned night after night. Erypmon told Allagrim to find some good men to take care of the animals and to send the women and children away until the ghost was defeated. He realised that Brunor had been possessed by some other thing before his death and it was this that was continuing the feud. Erypmon began to craft a stone that would allow him to send the ghost into the Outer Darkness. It was a reddish stone, common around his house. Erypmon carved signs into it and imbued it with a magic that could pierce the barriers into the Darkness. When he was done, he travelled with it to the farm of Allagrim.

As Erypmon expected, the ghost came again that night. The mage stood outside the main door of the building as it rampaged closer to the farmhouse. It saw him and came closer. Erypmon held out the stone as the ghost neared. The mage began to speak words of power and the stone glowed in his hand. The ghost screamed as it felt itself being drawn towards the stone. A gateway opened to the Darkness and the ghost passed through.

Erypmon told Allagrim that his farm and family were safe; the ghost would return no more. The grateful farmer sent good meat to the mage every winter. Erypmon kept the stone at his home. When in time he took an apprentice, he told the lad of the Stone's ability. The Stone continued to be passed along in this way.

Many years after the death of Erypmon, the stone was taken by the Council of Barakelth and used in a ritual to call forth the Xetal from the Outer Darkness. Then, after the Battle of the Plains of Harabrum, the Stone vanished. Grettin   y Gremnor of Svaltok travelled in the south two generations after the battle and was given the Stone by a dying mage, the last of those connected to the Council. Grettin knew the Stone for what it was and determined to hide it.

He travelled to the village of Greda in Tildeth. There he spoke to the elders and charged them to keep the Stone safe. They were to tell none of it except those who were to safeguard it and any skrel. If a Skrel were to ask for it, then they must give it up. The villagers took the Stone and held it safe as Grettin travelled to Skrelbard and informed the Skrelton of his deed.

This knowledge of the Stone of Erypmon was kept alive in Skrelbard. When traders began to carry stories of darkness and the name of the Council of Barakelth, the Skrelton acted. Gron ar Tolgath with Tharn y Relddu had found a way to destroy the artefacts of the Council years before. Now, the Skrelton sent Grok y Gremnor of Tolgath to find the Stone of Erypmon.

As Grok sailed to the south, other skrel were sent to gather information. Grok landed at the port of Brystan and made his way inland. He journeyed far and was met with interest everywhere he stayed. Most had never seen a skrel before. He travelled to Greda and spoke to the village elders. When he told them he needed the Stone of Erypmon, they took it from its hiding place of centuries and gave it to him. Thanking them for their work, he said goodbye and left the village.

Grok walked long after leaving the village; he camped just inside the borders of

Tildeth and left the land early the following day. Once clear of the mountains, he turned north, using a different route to the one he had entered by. He knew little of what powers were active in Grimevil and was wary of returning to Skrelbard directly in case of ambush.

In a Corbusian inn, he met a man by the name of Bruet Dence, one of the Freidyn. He had been told of Grok's presence by the innkeeper. Some travellers had told the innkeeper to take note of skrel and to send a message to a certain village if any were seen. The innkeeper distrusted the travellers and instead had told Dence of Grok.

Dence asked Grok for information about his journey. Grok asked him some questions; the answers proved he was a member of the Freidyn. In low voices, the two talked of the Stone and Grok's journey. Dence offered to travel with Grok to the border of Erein; he had heard word that others were searching for the Stone. Grok agreed, but charged Dence with carrying the Stone to Skrelbard if he were killed.

They set off the following morning, Dence had used what waning magic the Freidyn had to arrange lodgings along their road. They were in the second lodging when they heard of enemies. Two men, one old and one young, were on their trail seeking the Stone. Dence and Grok left before dawn. They stopped a short way down the road to eat breakfast. Whilst there, they saw a young man and an old man, both dressed in black, ride past.

They were certain that these were their pursuers, as it seemed unlikely that they had seen the two among the trees. The travellers continued, now aware of the possibility of ambush.

The sun was high when Dence and Grok heard hoofbeats approaching round a bend ahead of them. They moved to one side of the road and Grok untethered his axe from the pack on his back. Dence drew his sword and stood ready next to the Skrel. The same two men in black rode past. They reined in their equoths as Grok growled a challenge. Both jumped to the ground and drew weapons as they advanced. The younger man with his rapier was no match for a Skrel axe. The older attacked Dence with a sword. Neither had wounded the other when the assailant fell to the ground with his left hand pressed to his chest.

Grok held his axe at the man's throat as Dence searched him. The man was still alive but unconscious. The men were wearing small black brooches which showed them to be members of a Grimevillian group of assassins. Dence warned Grok that should the older man survive, the hunt would continue. Grok refused to kill the man who lay in the road. The assassins' equoths were still standing in the road. The four legged beasts of burden were known for being calm and would stand watching any fight short of a battle. Grok and Dence, with much prodding, persuaded them to move back up the road and continued on their journey.

At the border they parted, Grok gave Dence a carved sigil, which would show him to be a friend of the Skrel, able to call on skrel help when it should be needed.

Grok continued to Skrelbard. When he reached Tromok the Stone was destroyed by Friy y Relddu. This ends the story of the Stone of Erypmon.

As the young *larhwnen* finished speaking, his audience began applauding. He accepted a mug of water from Zen and sat down to one side.

"Where is Grok?" someone called.

"He is away from the village, he does not like being told how great he is!" another skrel shouted back. This prompted much laughter.

"What I want to know is how you got Grok to tell you all that," said Kris, to more laughter.

"Time and beer!" the young *larhwnen* replied.

Once the audience had quieted, another *larhwnen* stood up. "Friends, please refresh yourselves as we prepare for the tale of Pyra."

Chapter XIII

The winter continued. In Tolgath it was decided that Thenk and Grok would journey to Svaltok and speak to the leaders of Skrelbard. If a journey to the southern lands was required, it could be made in the better weather of Spring.

Grok and Thenk set off with snow still deep on the ground. Calon Gan stayed at Grok's house and spent more time talking to Zen and the *larhwnens.* Zen knew much of the history of the Council and told the Freidyn what he knew.

The Council had been in existence for many decades, seeking ways to power and contact with the Darknesses. No one who joined ever left and none who discussed their secrets lived. What was known came from informants whose lives were subsequently cut short. There were disquieting rumours in the southern lands when, without warning, the Xetal and their allies burst out of Grimevil. The lands of Corbus and Eltylon were unprepared and whole villages were swept away by humans and elves, some possessed by Xetal. The Council had long previous taken control of Grimevil, turning it from a peaceful and just land into a haven of darkness under a tyrannical King.

The Xetal and the Council found those people who exist in many lands, the ones willing to work with invaders and who ignore the death and destruction for the chance of power. More puppet governments were set up and the forces moved on, spreading north from Grimevil. Tyranth was the next to fall. The small land of Tildeth, sealing the pass that was its only access, was safe for the present. By this point, word had reached Skrelbard, Gamelen and Erein. Armies were prepared. The Order of Freidyn prepared to fight with the knowledge they had and allowed their magic users to cast the translation spells that enabled the leaders to talk to each other. The skrel crossed the Morleyd and united with the others. The Council forces were pressing into Erein when battle was joined.

It was only then that the forces of the North discovered the ability of the Xetal to possess intelligent beings. Men turned on their allies, others seemingly went mad and jumped off cliffs, or failed to defend themselves in the fight. The skrel were unaffected, but still the Northern forces were driven to withdraw.

Now was the time of the Freidyn. They had discovered a method of making the Xetal visible for short periods. The spell allowed them to observe that the Xetal had to be close to possess. They suspected that they could return the Xetal to their own dimension. Jenan Tor, the head of the Freidyn, spent much time talking with the other leaders; Krarg y Kreltor, Thanot of Erein and Rech of Gamelen. The ambassador of Tildeth sent a message via magic to say that his country would support any action they took.

At length a plan was made, which led to the Battle of the Plains of Harabrum. The skrel led the charge, their war howl spreading across the landscape like an advance guard. Distant from the risk of Xetal control, the humans, elves and Barances used crossbows and longbows as the Freidyn made their preparations.

A wave of energy blasted a hole in space and the Xetal were dragged through, back to their Outer Darkness.

Then the forces concentrated on the fighters loyal to the Council and their puppets. The magic users of the North and a small force from Tildeth joined in and eventually the Council was defeated. The inner Council were caught and imprisoned though some lesser members escaped, taking with them the implements that could summon the Xetal. Grimevil stayed dark and silent for many years. The ravaged lands of the other countries slowly healed and forms of responsible government took root.

Still, for many years after the lands were plagued by demons. They would appear from nowhere, cause havoc, and then disappear. As time went by the plague eased somewhat. The powers of the Freidyn and of the magic users faded with it. The Stone of Erypmon, the Spear of Pyra and the Hammer of Colwen passed beyond the ken of the southern peoples. The skrel and the Freidyn kept knowledge of them and what could happen should they once more appear.

When Grok and Thenk reached Svaltok, they discovered a disturbing rumour had reached there.

"If what we hear is true, then the Council has reformed," said Thark, when they met. He was the representative of Tolgath in Svaltok.

"Then the Skrelton should agree with Tolgath," said Thenk. "If the Council has reformed, we must be ready for the worst. When are you meeting?"

"Early tomorrow. Some have planned for this event since many years ago. We will confirm our plans shortly."

"Good." Grok was silent through the rest of the evening.

After they had eaten he went outside.

"Grok seems to have something on his mind," said Thark.

"Mmm," answered Thenk. "I am starting to sound like Grok!"

Grok stood under some trees on the edge of town. Various thoughts had been circulating through his mind since he had learned that the Council had reformed. The last war had been won, but this time? The Freidyn were reduced in number and less powerful. If the Council were allowed to reach Skrelbard, they could destroy the world without knowing it. They needed to be stopped before they became too powerful. Ideally, before they found the artefacts.

In Erein, three members of the Council of Barakelth were looking at the object lying on the table in front of them.

"Is it, Geoe?" asked Chene.

"It is, Chene," he replied.

"The Hammer of Colwen," breathed Tonb.

"The very hammer used by Colwen himself. Forged by the barances on the Isle of Eirlan and imbued with all the old magic Colwen had. To think that this hammer stove in the skulls of many skrel during the

War of Terenmar, serving Colwen when he ruled the land of Loegren," said Geoe.

Tonb stroked the hammer with a finger, his scarred face twisting into an smile. "How much blood has this shed as it found the enemies of Colwen and destroyed them? Truly the weapon of a ruler."

"But what of the others?" the elf asked.

"The Stone of Erypmon has been destroyed, Chene."

"What?" she raged.

"By the skrel."

"Those heathen barbarians! What of the Spear of Pyra?"

"That is what we must find now."

"I have no doubt that our enemies have the same idea."

Geoe's monkeyish face creased into a smile. "That is why we will begin searching now. There is one matter of Council lore that was never revealed to our enemies. The artefacts we used were merely the most powerful. There are others that can replace the Stone. When we have our power, there will be peace and stability."

Leku was lying at the base of a tree enjoying the feel of the sunshine on his face. The sun was growing stronger as the winter began to fade. As with all werewolves and werebrants, he could feel the currents of the world. Mostly just the gentle pulsing of life and sometimes the hint of huge forces as storms built over the Morfawr. It was a talent he had acquired along with his heightened sense of smell as if Nature, appalled at what it had done to him, was trying in some way to make up for it.

Before long the pulse would reach its strongest beat as life in Skrelbard roused from the slowness of winter. New life developing and plants growing as the snow disappeared. He was at peace with the world, as he had made his peace with his condition years ago. Others had not but his friends standing by him had been the key. They had been able to see past what happened at the full moon, and were prepared to defend the werewolf. A member of the Skrelton had been thrown through the wall of a hut by Grok when he tried to forcibly remove Leku from Tolgath. The incident being just one reason for the dislike some of the elder members of Tolgath had for Grok.

Something changed in the currents, Leku sat up as he felt it, trying to locate the source. It was faint, but ominous. He began to circle the tree. It came from the south. Leku's contentment faded as he tried to analyse the cause of the sinister ripple.

Grok and Thenk were drinking *cwr* while the Skrelton talked. Grok was drinking moodily and Thenk wondered how anyone could manage to drink anything in an aggressive way. Grok was a patient skrel, but he had a strong dislike of formality and those who talked without deciding. After two cups of *cwr*, they were asked into the chamber by Thark.

One of the skrel, elected as speaker for this occasion, rose from his seat.

"We are decided as one. We must prepare to defend against the actions of the Council of Barakelth and ask others to do the same.

"We have a request of you, Thenk al Krarg. Grok y Gremnor and Friy y Relddu have seen to the destruction of the Stone of Erypmon. We wish you to seek out the Hammer of Colwen and the Spear of Pyra. When they are in your hands, they must be destroyed for all time. Do you accept?"

"I do," Thenk replied, gravely.

"Then travel to the southern lands, speak to those who have knowledge and find the artefacts. Your success or failure will determine the future of our world."

Chapter XIV

In Tolgath, Zen was in the Longhouse alone when he saw a figure slip inside and move towards him, avoiding passing close to the small windows.

"Leku, what is it?" He knew it must be serious. With Grok not present, it had to be to drag the werewolf into the village.

Leku looked worried. "Something has changed, Zen. There is a sinister feel in the air."

"The Xetal?"

"No, not yet. I suspect the Council have reformed and achieved something."

"Are you sure?"

"No. The disturbance is not specific but it is an ill omen."

Unaware of developments elsewhere, Grok and Thenk were discussing matters in Svaltok.

"You will travel with me?" Thenk asked.

"Yes. Calon Gan will probably join us for part of the journey. Possibly Leku also."

"We should contact the Freidyn. Maybe one of them will know something about the artefacts, even if Calon Gan does not. Or at least suggest a place where they might be." Thenk paused. "Do you know how to destroy them?"

"Bring them back to Friy."

"Perhaps there is another way. Zen might know of something."

Thark walked into the room carrying a piece of parchment. "This is a request from the Skrelton for all in authority to help you. It is written in most of the languages, so it may be useful. It is unfortunate that we no longer have the ability to translate through magic as in the last war."

"Thanks," said Thenk, accepting it.

"Where will you go next?"

"Back to Tolgath and then travel south."

"Do you know where to begin your search?"

"Not yet. That is something we must discover. In our own history there might be a reference to the last known hiding place of the other two artefacts."

He knew that the location of the Stone of Erypmon would be no help. The Hammer and the Spear had disappeared in ages past and nothing was known of them

Days later, when Thenk and Grok reached home, they found Zen in a distracted frame of mind.

"Leku came to see me," he told them.

"What is wrong?" asked Grok.

"He felt something sinister has happened but did not know what."

"We need to leave soon," said Thenk. "The Skrelton has asked us to find and destroy the two remaining artefacts."

"I know of nothing that tells of their location. Calon Gan may have ideas, but you should look closer to home, Grok."

"What did he mean?" Thenk asked as they left the Longhouse.

"I think I know."

When Calon Gan returned to Grok's house after supper with Pola, he found the Skrel reading some parchments.

"They were written by my grandfather," he replied in answer to Calon Gan's question.

"You think they might help?"

"Zen suggested it. This is something the *larhwnens* don't deal with, it is not known as truth but just speculation. He felt it was important enough to pass down through the family. It is one reason I was taught to read."

Gan left Grok alone and started to make *cwr.* The skrel continued to read.

Things are not always what they seem when tales are passed down, Gron had written. *Fiction mingles with allegory which mixes with history. There are a number of locations which could be resting places. Most are known to others, but Beddcrul in Erein, Monstrea on the coast of Corbus and Travan in Tyranth would appear to be most likely. This is gleaned from hints in old writings and the tales of our larhwnens.*

The actual locations were carefully hidden by those who survived the battle. They left word with trusted scribes who recorded the hiding places for those who would follow the Council's lead. Through the years the stories were lost. I hope that it will not be necessary to trace the locations and prevent the artefacts from being used during the lifetimes of my children or my grandchildren.

With destinations in mind, Grok, Thenk and Leku made preparations for the journey. Calon Gan decided to travel with them as far as his home in Penmin on the coast of Erein. There he would do research while the Skrel investigated Beddcrul.

The weather was still wintry the night before they left. Grok stood outside the Longhouse and looked up at the stars as his mind walked along unfamiliar paths. He normally looked forward to travelling; his wanderlust could be subdued but never removed. Yet, this time was different. He was worried about leaving Tolgath. As he mused on the events occurring in the world, he sensed Zen joining him. They stood in silence for some minutes as the aurora spread across the sky.

"You are concerned," said Zen. It was not a question.

Grok looked up at the lights.

"To set out on a journey that you may not return from is daunting."

Grok's eyes flicked briefly in Zen's direction and returned to the sky.

"The universe is not concerned with fairness. There is no certainty that you will return home. But if you do not leave, there may be no home for any of us."

Grok continued watching the aurora. He supposed that everyone tasked with such a mission would have doubts. He knew he was different than when he had fought Death. Then, he had hope that things could be better. Now, he hoped to prevent them from becoming worse. There was only one thing he could do. He turned and walked into the Longhouse with Zen following.

Chapter XV

Kris, Pola and Zen were at the Longhouse to see the travellers off on their journey. "Here are some medicinal herbs and preparations," said Pola, as she handed Grok a small package. "You are travelling to dangerous territory. They may well be useful."

"Thanks," Grok replied, putting the package into one of his many pockets.

"Do you know when you will be back?" Kris asked.

"We hope to be here before the winter, if all goes well," Thenk told him.

"I will take care of your houses while you are travelling. If any work is needed, it will be done. It is the least Tolgath can do for you. Your places as well,

Leku."

"Thank you, Kris. Though I suspect others will try to destroy them," the werewolf said gloomily.

"That is why I asked for your possessions," Zen told him. They will be held safe at my house. I have asked two of the woodskrel I can trust, to inform us of anything unusual there. We will do what we can."

"Thanks."

As they were making final checks of their packs and Grok was examining his axe, Dak appeared.

"What is that doing here?" he shrilled, pointing at Leku.

Gan heard an odd swishing noise as Grok's axe swung through the air and stopped just by Dak's throat.

"Leku is working with us to end the threats of the Council and the Xetal. He is helping to save this village as well as your life. Remember that," Grok growled, his voice deeper than normal.

He held the axe in place, forcing Dak to move closer to Leku to get away. The skrel traded glances as Dak left.

"You will be doing the talking, Thenk?" Zen asked.

"Yes, Zen. I will have to be the diplomat."

"We should go," growled Grok. "*Throm tel!*"

"Always the short goodbye," murmured Pola.

So, the quartet left on their journey. Three days later they were in Tromok, having taken the easier route through the pass of Kergol due to Calon Gan's age. They were warmly welcomed at the Skrelgrun Inn and spent the night there before they left on the first southbound ship of the season.

Friy came to see them at the Inn. "I heard word of your journey," he said. "Will you bring the artefacts here to be destroyed?"

"We plan to.," said Thenk.

"When the Hammer of Colwen is found you can give it to the Freidyn. They will have to means to destroy it."

"Do you know how?" Thenk asked Calon Gan.

" I do not, yet others may. We have areas we concentrate on with our studies, there is no one Freidyn who can know all that the Order knows. I will find the one who has that knowledge," the old man replied.

"What about the Spear?" Thenk asked Friy.

"Gron and Tharn left specific instructions on how to destroy it. Before midsummer we will have that ability. Bring it to me and the Spear will be no more." He paused. "If the Council are close to taking the Spear there is another way to destroy it, one that Pyra himself provided. The Spear will be destroyed should it be used to kill a skrel."

There was a silence as he finished speaking. They all considered that possibility and how it would be achieved if necessary.

"Good luck, all of you," Friy said, as he stood up and moved to the bar.

Grok sat silently as his friends began to talk again. Death would allow him to keep one life in the world, that life could be the one that destroyed the Spear. But the life would have to be taken first, by one of their group. Even if the Council did not know what effect killing a skrel would have on the Spear, there was no guarantee they would use it for such. The room seemed to grow darker and colder as he realised what must happen if they were to destroy the Spear without the help of Friy. That destruction would also mean the destruction of the Council. As Pure Land had paid for the death of his family, so the Council would pay for the death of his friend.

The following morning they boarded the *Edescon*, the vessel bound for Grimsbal. As the ship left the dock the skrel stayed on deck, watching as the mountains of Skrelbard slowly receded. Grok decided that, if he did return, he wanted to spend some time in Tolgath.

The winds began to increase as the sun set that evening and the sea became choppy. The master was not concerned. It was common for strong winds to blow towards the coasts of Gamelen and Erein at this time of year. Thenk did not eat much at the evening meal and retired to his cabin early. When Leku went in later he found his cabinmate asleep in the swaying hammock.

Thenk was more lively the following day when the winds abated. He talked to Calon Gan about Beddcrul, where they would begin their search for the Spear.

"It is not a place that I know well. There is a small village and an hour's walk from there are some ruins. Parts of the ruins are very old and some are more recent. The local people have stories of tunnels underneath the ruins full of treasure and monsters." He smiled. "Such stories are common wherever there are old ruins. If there is anything there, I would think the ancient section is where to look."

Leku was on deck, standing next to Grok. The skrel were leaning on the bulwark, watching the ocean. "It has been a long time since I last left Skrelbard. Now I think I understand some of what motivates you," the werewolf said.

Grok smiled. "Someone in Corbus once told me that it is better to travel than arrive."

The rest of the journey was uneventful. Within two hours of arriving in Grimsbal, they were sailing south to Penmin. The journey would take several days to complete, the small ship stayed close to the shore. Late on the second day the winds increased sharply, sending Thenk to his hammock again. The captain steered the ship into a sheltered anchorage, where she stayed for some hours.

The hills inland were low and rolling. They showed no signs of the snow that still blanketed Skrelbard. The new growths of spring were not apparent from the sea but winters were obviously less severe here.

As the ship approached Penmin, its home port, the passengers and crew watched dark storm clouds that were nearing the coast. Grok noticed that Calon Gan was looking concerned.

"That is not a good sign?" Grok asked.

"I have spent much of my life on this coast," the old man said in reply. "I know the moods of the weather. That is a large storm. It is well that we will be in harbour before it arrives."

The winds had begun to freshen as their ship was secured to the dock in Penmin's natural harbour. Calon Gan led the way through the narrow streets, pausing to buy food, before walking on a path that led up onto the cliffs. His house was a low stone building with a sod roof that looked out across the village of Penmin to the sea.

Dry firewood was stacked up near the fireplace and Thenk quickly began making a fire. Calon Gan apologised for the lack of space, explaining that he didn't get many visitors. Of the three rooms, only the kitchen was empty of scrolls, books and parchments.

Leku looked out of the window. "A nice metaphor," he muttered as he looked at the dark clouds. A kettle was set on the fire and *cwr* was prepared. In spite of his guests' offer Calon Gan insisted on preparing supper himself. Grok was feeling restless, so he left Calon Gan to prepare and walked back down to the village.

The wind buffeted him and blew his cloak around him as he walked into the narrow valley. He had not visited the place before and was impressed at the way the Penminians had constructed their village in the available space. The valley had a natural harbour and a stone jetty had been built for extra protection. A small vessel running ahead of the storm entered the harbour as Grok joined the watching crowd. His knowledge of this particular Ereinian dialect was slight, but it seemed that this was the last of the boats from Penmin to return. The crowd began to disperse as the boat was moored. Grok was left looking at the white horses on the Morfawr. This was still not the main storm and the sea was already looking dangerous.

As the first rain made landfall, he turned back to

the main part of the village. He was walking along the narrow main road when a stranger stopped him.

"You *et* here *maltan Fraten* Calon Gan?"

"Yes," replied Grok, hoping he had understood the man's meaning.

The stranger handed him a package. "This arrived *relas* winter. I am Kalgan."

"*Mer dan*," replied Grok, using the inland dialect.

The man replied with something cheerful sounding in Penmish and hurried off. Grok took the path up the cliffs at a fast pace, hurrying to get out of the rain. The wind had strengthened so that it rattled the door in its frame as Grok lowered a bar across it.

"Kalgan had this for you," he told Calon Gan, handing over the parcel.

"He has been a good friend of the Freidyn," Gan said as he unwrapped the parcel. "Ah. It is a copy of the *Amgolian Telcortan*."

Grok looked at the book in Calon Gan's hands. It was a series of parchments bound together in a skin cover. "That is good?"

"I forget, my friend, you are not well schooled in the arcane mysteries. The originals of these manuscripts pre-date the Council of Barakelth and contain the antecedents of the rituals used by the Council. They may contain information that the Council tried to suppress, thus it may be of great value to us. I believe that whoever gave the book to Kalgan did not fully understand its importance. Otherwise they would hardly have left it with a stranger. Now that I have it I must use the spell of binding, that will prevent it from leaving this house."

"You can use that magic?" Grok asked.

"There is still enough in the world for such a simple spell. I am no mage, yet I can perform such minor magic. The writings in this book are some of the most ancient known."

Grok was spared a detailed history of the book when Leku announced that the supper was almost ready. The four ate well and talked more of the coming journey to Beddcrul.

"I would suggest four days to get there, knowing how fast you can walk," said Calon Gan. "Possibly five if the weather remains poor. The ruins are past the village as you travel along the road. If you do need to stay at the inn, only stay one night. Never tell anyone your real destination. Three skrel travelling together will attract attention but Beddcrul is on a major road so that may allay suspicion. We do not know what intelligence the Council has so they may be looking for the Spear as well.

"The ruins may take some time to search, so you ought to camp there. Unless you take some days over the ruins, there is no time for you to reach the next village and return in that time. Do not pass through Beddcrul on your return, travel through the countryside. It would start talk that may hurt our cause, if you were seen. I will study while you are gone and, hopefully, will discover something of use to us by the time you return."

A short way down the coast a cowled figure stood on the windswept cliffs, its attention focused on a small boat that had been caught in the storm. It was being driven towards the rocks as the two figures on board struggled to control their vessel. The figure watched calmly as the elf and human neared the end of their lives. Not long until my day off, he thought thankfully. With luck the weather will be better. The wind carried the noise of the wreck up the cliff. The words Death spoke were lost in the wind and the rain. Then, he turned away.

Chapter XVI

The weather was calm and mild in Breltag, Grimevil's capital city. The Lonskat of Grimevil, the leader of the land, paced the terrace waiting for his late visitor. He knew the garden was well guarded, still he watched carefully for assassins. Ten minutes later, she walked across the gardens with the grace typical of the elves. They greeted each other.

"Well? What have you decided?" asked the visitor.

"*Elcon renda un pace.*"

"*Un pace deteum parla.*"

"I have done what you requested of me," said the Lonskat.

"Yes. You and your land are now pledged to the Council. We cannot yet openly declare ourselves, not until we have the Spear. This time there must be no mistakes. The Freidyn, the skrel, and all who oppose us will be crushed. Then the Council of Barakelth will rule and there will be peace and stability!"

A young man hidden in the shadows of the garden now slipped away and returned to his home. There, he began to assemble the necessary potions and herbs for a communication spell. The Freidyn in Corbus had to be told of the union between Grimevil and the Council.

As Thenk stepped outside the following morning, he noticed that the winds had eased. The worst of the storm had passed. He looked down at the sea and saw a body that had washed ashore. Not far away from him, a rough path led down to the natural seawater pool. Thenk neared the corpse and saw that it was an elf, still clutching a waterproofed package in one hand. The skrel prised the fingers open and pulled out the waterproofed packet.

It contained a parchment written in a strange script wrapped around an ornate seal. There were no clues to the elf's identity, nothing in his clothes. The tide was ebbing so he pulled the body above the strand line. It would be safe there until someone from Penmin could take it for whatever rites the elves preferred.

When he reached the house the others were sitting around drinking *cwr*. He avoided speaking to Grok as it looked like his friend hadn't finished his first cup. Grok was not a skrel who liked mornings and preferred to be left alone until he felt fully awake.

"Do you know what these are?" he asked, handing the package to Calon Gan.

"Where did you get this?" Calon Gan asked.

"There is a dead elf at the base of the cliff. Probably got caught in the storm, though I saw no wreckage," Thenk told him.

"It is the sign of the Council of Barakelth. This parchment carries the oath which members must take on joining the Council. They must be recruiting. Elves must be allied with the Council once more."

"Were they before?"

"All races here, excepting the skrel, were represented on the Council. We should not be surprised that elves have rejoined." He paused, "I must send a message to Luden Kul." He picked up a piece of paper and began to write.

Thenk looked at Grok's mug. It was now almost full again, so it was safe to start talking.

"How did you sleep?"

"Well. What is the plan for today?" Grok replied, taking a sip from the steaming mug.

Leku drained his mug and stretched. "We need to get organised for Beddcrul."

"We have most of what we need. Food is the main thing," said Thenk.

"When is the full moon?" Grok asked.

"Six nights from now."

Gan finished his letter and folding it up, sealed it with wax. "I must take this to Estone the messenger. We can then visit the market and buy your provisions. You will be able to leave tomorrow morning to take advantage of the most daylight for travelling."

Chapter XVII

They set off after breakfast. Calon Gan told them

that he would send help if they were not back within ten days. They left him to his studies and walked down into Penmin to join the road, which meandered across the landscape. After four miles it joined the road to Canatel which led through Beddcrul.

Spring had arrived, birds sang and flowers were appearing. As usual there was little talk as they walked. The main road was paved and the verges were kept well trimmed,which made it harder for the occasional bandits to ambush travellers. Not that they would have bothered three armed skrel.

Grok was thinking about the ruins of Beddcrul and what could be waiting for them there. He knew from past experience that a life-threatening situation could erupt out of a casual inspection or just on a walk along a road. *When one travelled, there was more chance of encountering a demon that had slipped through from the Outer Darkness than if you stayed at home. Though if the priests were right and there were gods in charge, they were a bunch of incompetent maniacs.*

The weather remained fair for the rest of the day and they made good time. The sun was still high as they passed through a small village, so they decided to camp further along the road. When the sun neared the horizon, they found a suitable campsite away from the road. A belt of trees blocked the view of any travellers on the road and a clear stream ran alongside it.

"Should we keep a guard?" asked Thenk.

"We should be safe enough," Leku replied.

"I do not think the Council has enough agents yet,"

growled Grok. "But we should be careful closer to Beddcrul."

"The problem is that we do not have much to go on," Thenk commented. "The Council are around somewhere, but we do not know where. They might have agents or they might not. They might open the gates to the Outer Darkness, but for what?"

"Power. That is the usual reason," Leku growled.

"Power to make everyone think like you, to have no freedom, and to call it peace," Grok rumbled, lower than normal.

"Every time you talk that deep, I know someone is in trouble," said Thenk, with a playful jab at Grok's arm.

Shortly after dawn, they moved on. The day passed uneventfully and they rested at an isolated inn.

They were delayed by bandits on a quiet stretch of road the following day. The bandits jumped out before realising who the travellers were. On seeing three skrel glaring at him, their leader looked extremely uncomfortable. He came from the south where the skrel were referred to in dark tones, but rarely encountered. The skrel said nothing while the bandits waited for their leader to speak. Eventually, he managed to find his voice, but he spoke to his companions.

"That, lads, is how your average bandit gang works. Jump out at a small group of travellers. That is why we need to be looking at the sides of the road all the time." He smiled at the skrel, who grinned back with more fangs than the leader liked.

"Anti-bandit squad, sirs. Just training 'em up.

Please, carry on."

"Sorry to bother you," said one of the others, who had been eyeing the axe on Grok's pack.

The skrel continued on until they had rounded a bend. Then they started to laugh.

"Anti-bandit squad!" howled Leku. "That's a good one."

Further along the road, they passed another group of travellers and warned them about the bandits. Thenk suggested they mention that there were more skrel coming along just behind them.

It was early in the morning the following day that clouds began to obscure the sun, which had been shining for most of their journey. Rain and wind followed. It was a bedraggled trio who entered the village of Branculen that afternoon. They estimated it would be at least another day to Beddcrul. With shelter between the villages probably non-existent, Grok scanned the sky. "I think this weather is set for the day."

"You think we should stop here?" Leku asked. Grok shrugged and continued to look at the clouds.

"We are all soaked. If we stay, we will just lose a couple of hours start on the ruins," Thenk pointed out.

"I agree, we should stay here if we can. Grok?"

"Sure. We can dry out a bit."

They continued down the main street and looked for a place to stay. The village was small and apparently only had one inn. Thenk went inside the inn to ask about rooms. The obliging landlord had three rooms available, food included but not beer.

Thenk called the others over and after handing over some gold they went to their rooms.

Some time later, Grok was in dry clothes and his wet ones were steaming in front of a fireplace. The hills visible through the window were shrouded with mist as the rain continued to fall. He was thinking about what Leku had said about the Council wanting power. Power for what exactly? Control the world and pretend you are doing something good. Then someone else wants your power and wars start. With access to the Outer Darkness, they could access the old magic and end the world. Where did the Xetal fit in, if at all? Was there some force deliberately weakening the barriers or was it a natural process?

Grok had an ancient piece of parchment at his home. His grandfather had acquired it and added a translation into Skrel. He had left it for his grandson with the suggestion to see Zen about it. It had been, apparently, dictated by a man called Frak. He had accessed the Freidyn's view of the future and looked further than the Freidyn had dared, many times further forward. He had seen a future where everything had ceased to exist. Not only no skrel and no elves, but no world, no light. Eternal silent darkness. Even Death had ceased to exist.

The vision had driven him to the edge of sanity. The parchment had been written by a scribe to whom Frak had told his story, just before he jumped off the highest tower of the Fortress of Kalenwen. Could these be the first signs of that future? The Council able to take control of the world and attack Skrelbard? The old Council's hatred of the skrel was well known, they had openly talked of destroying the skrel. For all their knowledge, they still did not know how important the skrel were to the world.

Grok's dark thoughts were interrupted by Leku who told him that there were hot drinks waiting. He shook off his dark mood and followed his lycanthropic friend downstairs.

The drinks were malted milk and warming, which was their main concern. The rain beat against the windows as the skrel relaxed in front of the fire. The inn was quiet at this time of day and the innkeeper inclined to be talkative. "What brings skrel to our part of the kingdom?" he asked.

"We are travelling further, beyond Beddcrul. There is a man there called Dylanth who lives along the road," Thenk replied. "He is interested in trade with Skrelbard."

"I cannot say I know the name, but even I cannot claim to know everyone in Erein, eh?" the innkeeper replied in Ereinian, the inland dialect.

They all laughed, even Leku who had barely followed a word.

"There have been strange tales from down south in Corbus though. We get some merchants who travel from that way, see? Some old watchtower just fell apart. One day it was up on the hill like normal. Next morning, pile of stones. It did not fall down either. Folks heard it coming apart like something was pushing from the inside. Then, in the mountains," he lowered his voice, "three bodies found in a pass. Not all there either." He spoke again in his previous tone. "There are strange things happening these days. I must go and see how my missus is doing in the kitchen. The girl who helps us has the shaking sickness. The trials of an innkeeper."

He left the fire and disappeared though a door into the back of the inn. Grok quickly translated what the innkeeper had told them for Leku.

"I would say, is there anything to it?" Leku said, "but it is too easy to see signs everywhere."

"A traveller I once met said he knew of a country where the favoured curse translates as 'May you live in interesting times'," Grok commented. "Who is Dylanth?"

"I have no idea. I just thought of the name and hoped he would not know someone like that."

As dusk deepened, the inn began to fill up with travellers and locals. The skrel joined others at the long table where a large meal was spread out.

"The innkeeper has his own garden," a merchant next to Thenk observed. "I always arrange to stop here when I am on this road. No better food between Canatel and Penmin."

The merchant was correct, the meal was excellent. Most of the travellers stayed downstairs afterwards. It was a good-natured group and a couple of the locals got up on a table and began singing. At the urging of the crowd, two humans in the brightly coloured dress of Tildeth stood up and sang some old songs from their country. Then some Algholians sang.

It was inevitable that someone would ask the skrel to join in. Thenk stepped up, thrust forward by the others. Leku hated being the centre of attention and Grok claimed his singing voice was like a wolf with a bad throat.

Thenk was finishing his second song, a slow one about a skrel warrior at a watchtower, when Leku whispered to Grok.

"The human by the bar with fair hair, next to the two elves."

"I see him."

"There is something wrong about him."

Grok did not ask how he knew, he had learned to trust Leku when his friend detected something wrong. The werewolf could sense things most could not.

"More beer?" he asked, draining his own tankard.

Thenk had started singing a drinking song as Grok moved up to the bar, next to the suspicious human. The barmaid was busy.

"Good song, eh? " he said to the man, with a grin full of more sharp teeth than seemed possible.

"Yes." The stranger, freezingly polite, seemed put out by having a skrel talk to him.

"Three pints of your local beer please," Grok asked the barmaid.

As the human turned away from him, Grok noticed a small chain round the human's wrist. It was attached to a small engraved copper disc lying on the bar, he casually put his hand on it as he waited for the beer. The stranger moved away from Grok. His hand was jerked back as the chain became taut.

"Sorry," apologised Grok, lifting his hand. "That is an interesting design there."

"An artistic work of my own," the stranger said coldly, walking away as Grok picked up his beers.

"You were right," he told Leku as he handed him a tankard. Thenk was still at the front of the crowd, who congratulated him on his performance. "He is with the Council, I recognised the symbol on a copper disc he wears."

The werewolf glanced round to see where the human was. "Do you think he knows why we are here?"

"Probably not. He is leaving, though. Let him be, we know he is with the Council. He may not know why we are here and I do not want to start anything now. Three skrel attacking a human for no reason will start far more talk than three skrel travelling." A torrent of rain entered as the stranger slipped out the door.

"There was a Council member here," Leku told Thenk when he rejoined them. "Might not mean anything."

The man did not reappear that night, nor was he seen by the skrel the following morning. The weather seemed to be set in a dismal, threatening pattern; the lowering clouds were still present as they left the village.

Chapter XVIII

They made good time to Beddcrul, a small village with few large buildings. They lingered only long enough to buy some provisions before continuing along the road.

About a mile out of the village were the ruins: haunted, said some; cursed, said others. They had been abandoned after the Xetal War but had been home to a mage guild. As the magic faded so did the guilds. The places they once called home were avoided. The new road kept its distance but there were still traces of the slabs that had formed the highway into the ruins.

Not trusting the sparse cover near the junction, the skrel continued along the road until it entered a small wood. Then they moved into the trees and using the cover, doubled back to the ruins. The buildings had been very solid when new and most were still standing, even though the roofs and floors had collapsed. The ghost stories had kept the villagers from using it as a quarry.

They set up camp in the shelter of a wall that still had some roof intact. It would shield their fire from the view of travellers on the road and there was a well with drinkable water.

After some searching, they found two entrances to underground passageways. If the Spear of Pyra was in Beddcrul, it probably would be underground. The guilds were known to have favoured building underground vaults to secure their money and valuable magic items.

"This is the best I could do," said Grok. He added more firewood to the pile that Thenk and Leku had collected. "Everything else is too wet. Are you ready to start searching?"

"How far do the tunnels go?" asked Thenk.

"Calon Gan did not know," answered Grok. "It could take some time."

"The full Moon is tonight," Leku reminded them.

"Then, we should take a look down there now and see if we can find any trace of the Spear."

Thenk rummaged in his pack and produced three torches. One he stuck in his belt, the others, he lit. "When they start to fail, we come out."

With Thenk and Leku holding the torches, they walked down the worn stone steps and into the passageway. The meagre daylight crept in a short way before it was swallowed by the underground darkness. What dampness there was had entered down the steps, the passage was well-drained. The ceiling was low, forcing the skrel to crouch as they walked along.

They walked carefully along the corridor. Thenk was first, Grok just behind him, and Leku at the rear. The passageway went on for some distance before they saw rooms. Most were bare and empty, but some had remnants of furniture. The wall hangings still present were moth-eaten and faded. Grok dragged a couple of old chairs into the passage to use as firewood.

The Skrel had not completed their search as the torches began to fail. They moved back to the surface, picking up the chairs on their way. All three were relieved to be in the open air again. The underground rooms, though free of noxious vapours, had an oppressiveness they disliked.

The rain had started again while they were underground, so they sat near the fire and made *cwr*. No rain fell on them, but the air was chilly and damp. As they drank, they discussed their next move.

"We could go back now," said Thenk, "but there is

no way to see when the sun will set. Dark could come without us knowing."

"We can go back," Leku said. "I can sense the influence of the moon before I change. We can return to the surface in time."

The others agreed. They lit more torches and returned to the passages.

As they searched, it became clear that people had lived in the subterranean area. There were old clothes and furniture containing cooking utensils in one room. It seemed that any valuables had been taken a long time ago, with no sign of anything that could be the Spear of Pyra. There were no books left, or anything else that might form a clue to the Spear's whereabouts.

The final chamber they examined was of most interest. It had been ransacked, but the one who had done it was still there. A skeleton in the torn remains of leather armour lay on the floor with an arrow between two ribs. Leku sniffed the end of the arrow. "This was tipped with poison."

"Can you tell which one?" asked Thenk.

"A plant similar to valweed," the werewolf replied, then sneezed. "Valweed always does that to me."

The bag the adventurer had been carrying was still on the floor. Thenk rummaged through it. "Nothing spear-like in here. Some silver, quite a bit of gold. Look at this!" He pulled a small statue of a bird from the bag and showed it to the others.

"Is that real copper?"

"Looks like it." Thenk examined the statue in the torchlight. "You see those traces of green? That happens to old copper."

"If it is solid, then I can see why people talked about vast treasure here."

Thenk kept hold of the copper statue. Grok moved off to search further and unearthed two books, the language was unintelligible, but he kept them. Any information could be useful.

"Gron said that there was only a chance the artefacts were here. We should check on the surface before we leave," Grok commented.

"Maybe mage guilds were not considered trustworthy by the Council. What is it?" Thenk asked Leku who was carefully examining a wall.

"I can smell rain. There must be a hidden door here," the werewolf replied.

He pressed likely looking stones and eventually a section swung open. A gust of air swept in with the fresh dampness of rain not the foetid dampness of underground. Leku picked up a rusted helmet and threw it onto the flagstone in the doorway. A large spike flew across the gap and into a socket on the opposite wall. They looked at each other and cautiously moved through. After a few feet there were steps leading up. The exit was heavily overgrown, but they soon emerged in the woods not far from the ruins.

"A handy way out," said Grok.

The dusk was deep. Leku looked around.

"You two go back to the camp. I will be along." he paused. "Later."

They split up. Leku moved a short way into the trees and watched his friends walk back to the ruins.

The change would come soon.

Grok and Thenk prepared a meal when they reached camp. Grok set the books aside for later study.

"He will back to normal in the morning," Grok said. "We are safe."

"I know."

They ate supper in silence.

Leku huddled against the damp bark of a tree feeling the tingling spread over his skin. The physical effects of transformation were not as bad as the mental effects. The feeling of his mind being swallowed by something else, something so different from Leku that he could never understand it. He felt a million pinpricks as the fur pushed its way through his skin. His nails, like all skrel's, fairly claw-like, lengthened and grew sharper. His face extended into a muzzle, the teeth sharper.

The black cloud washed over his mind. Strange thoughts often not seeming to be his own, flooded in. The wood around him formed into a mass of odours as the green leaves turned to grey. An overwhelming urge to hunt swept over him. In the small area of lighted sanity on an endless darkened plain, Leku prepared to fight. Not against whatever prey might present itself, but to fight against the forces that wanted him to join them. The forces that promised long life, but one spent in the shadows. This bestial aspect to be dominant, Leku as a prisoner in his own form, able to look out and witness the aberrant body carrying out acts loathsome to him, unable to stop it.

Acting out not the dark side of skrel nature, but the dictates of things that moved forever in the shadows at the edge of the world. Things that made the Council seem as children in a crib. Things that every werewolf and werebrant were condemned to fight against at every full moon, to fight to remain who they were. Those who failed became agents of the power. Those who were killed by silver before they lost were consumed by the things, strengthening the darkness even as the living sought to destroy it. Think of Grok, of Thenk. His friends who were his anchor to the world. Who would appear to him, so he thought, supporting him in his fight.

Fresh meat, must eat! Fresh blood. No! Find Grok. Need help. Grok, help!

Seated by the fire, Thenk looked out into the darkness that hid Leku.

"I never asked you," he said, almost to himself.

"What?" Grok asked, looking up from the book he was flipping through.

"I know you and Leku were friends before he was bitten. Why did you stay loyal when others did not."

"Like me, he is obviously different to most other skrel."

Thenk frowned as he attempted to work out Grok's meaning. "You are not that different."

"You have known me so long that you do not see it."

"See what?" Thenk asked, more confused.

Grok pointed to his eyes. "How few of us have blue eyes?" he asked. "In Tolgath, no one else but me. Children notice things like that, they were never scared or hostile. I was known as the one with blue eyes, the one different to everyone else. The one some of the more superstitious elders worry about."

"Being a werewolf is slightly more different than having an unusual eye colour."

"He is still physically different," Grok paused, "some of the time. Above all, he is a friend. Not someone to be abandoned for something that happened to them."

"Shhh. I heard something out there," Thenk whispered.

Grok put down the book and picked up his axe, which was lying by his pack. Thenk unsheathed his sword as the noises approached. A half-rotted corpse entered the firelight, followed by two skeletons. All were armed with swords. The skrel jumped into the fight. A blow from Grok's axe disarmed a skeleton and he attacked the corpse as Thenk took on the other skeleton.

The corpse made a moaning sound as the axe bit deeply into its side but flailed at Grok with his sword. The axe's next stroke took off its sword arm, decapitating it with the third. Thenk's assailant was losing bones rapidly as they were broken by his sword. A well aimed swing removed the skull and the skeleton collapsed.

Both skrel now took on the second skeleton. It had retrieved its sword and was swinging wildly, forcing both skrel to keep dodging. They were unable to deal a serious blow. Thenk whistled and using his eyes, indicated to Grok that he should try and flank the skeleton. Grok nodded and Thenk took a step back.

The skeleton followed him, allowing Grok to slip behind it. The axe removed its sword arm, Thenk's sword removed the skull. With the attackers defeated, they smashed the skeleton's skulls to stop them being reanimated.

Then a demon leapt into view. It was a reddish colour, slightly taller than the skrel, with long horns on either side of its head. It carried a shield in one long-clawed hand and a sword in the other.

Caught by surprise, Thenk was unready when the sword swung at him. The blade grazed the back of his sword hand, causing his grip to slacken. "Grok!" The demon's shield hit him on the side of the head, sending him to the ground. He looked up at the demon dazedly as it raised his sword for a coup de grace. The sword came down, missing Thenk as the demon staggered to the left. Grok's axe had slammed into its leg, releasing a gout of foul smelling black blood.

The fiend turned its attention to the new enemy and sword clashed against axe, then axe hit shield. Grok was used to fighting with a two handed axe but this demon matched him blow for blow.

Both combatants were bloodied when a growling noise came from behind the demon. A large, furred monster jumped on its back. Huge, sharp teeth were bared as the creature's long claws dug into the skin of its prey. Grok knew it was Leku. The werewolf's teeth fastened on the creature's sword arm allowing Grok to dodge a blow. Then the werewolf's paws gripped the demon's head and broke its neck with a swift movement.

As the demon fell, the werewolf began to lunge at Grok yet held itself back. His eyes showed the internal battle raging. His muzzle wrinkled as he snarled before forcing his lips to cover the teeth. Then he turned and ran into the darkness.

Some distance away stood the human they had seen at the inn and an elf. The human ceased his hand gestures and sagged as the demon was killed by Leku.

"They have defeated the creatures I sent."

"For such an barbaric race, they do seem to have knack for defeating the plans of their superiors," the elf replied. "We must try again."

"In the morning, Alron. With the magic so weak I must rest before I can summon demons and the dead once more."

"Very well. But they must be killed."

"You fear that they will find the Spear of Pyra?"

"They are skrel. Whether they find the Spear or not, they are our enemies. The skrel will never support our bid to bring stability and peace. They helped defeat us before and would destroy the artefacts if they could. My people regard them as little more than animals, yet they will not take the necessary step. When the Council regains power we will ensure peace by destroying the skrel."

Not hearing sounds of anything else lurking in the darkness, Grok turned his attention to Thenk.

"You killed it?" Thenk asked as he opened his eyes.

"No, Leku did. Wait there."

Apart from his hand Thenk had no serious injuries

and just needed some rest. With practised skill. Grok bound up his friend's hand. "Pola taught you well," Thenk said as he examined his hand, flexing his fingers. Grok dragged the corpses away from the camp. The rain was falling again, and there were no signs of animal life immediately outside the camp.

"Leku?" Thenk asked, as Grok returned to the fire.

"No sign of him."

"Grok, you are covered in blood."

"Mainly from that demon. I just have a scratch."

"If someone took your arm off, you would say it was a scratch."

"You are good now?" asked Grok, ignoring the jibe.

"Yes."

Grok left the shelter and stood outside in the rain, allowing the clean water to wash the blood off him.

Thenk had slipped into a light doze when he returned to the fire. He set a pot of water to boil and changed into dry clothes. He hoped Leku would make it through the night unscathed. The thought that they might not make it back to Skrelbard resurfaced. For a moment, he found himself wishing that he could return to his old life. But no, he had accepted that there could be no going back after Aula and Krarg had died. With clothes drying around him, he turned his attention back to the books.

The script was entirely unfamiliar, he had seen books written in a number of languages, but never this one. It seemed as if these books were of no use. He took a sip of hot *cwr* and turned another page. He frowned, this one had two scripts on it. He looked closer, the left-hand side of the page was the strange script. The right-hand side was a more familiar script, he looked at it. Some words were familiar, it was Tyranthian. Presumably, the Tyranthian was a translation of the unknown language. He could get by in Tyranth, but after asking for directions or ordering food and beer, his knowledge of the language was limited. He had never spent enough time in the land to learn more. Reading through the Tyranthian translation yielded too little to make sense. He looked through more pages in hopes the unknown scribe had translated into more languages, but was disappointed.

Grok set the book down and rested his head against the stone wall behind him. He was still for some minutes, listening to the rain. Behind the blue eyes his mind was working. The Freidyn had members in Tyranth, others may be able to speak the language and translate the unknown. He did not know how long it would take, but it could be weeks. They would have to travel elsewhere, searching for the Spear without waiting to learn what knowledge the books held. With the books in the hands of the Freidyn, the information they held would be kept from the Council. Unless, other copies could have been made. He thumped his clenched fist against his thigh in irritation. When he hunted a boar or a deer, he could lie in wait and let the arrow fly at precisely the moment for it to kill swiftly. There could be no ambush for the Council without more knowledge, they had to be disarmed instead. But they were also looking for their weapons, it was a race.

He growled in annoyance at himself, now was the time to rest. There was a journey ahead, yet his mind would not stop trying to outwit the rest of the world. He knew sleep would not come yet, so he picked up the other book and began to read it.

The sun was shining, although wanly, when Thenk awoke. He felt clear-headed though his cut was painful. He was building up the fire when a bedraggled Leku joined them.

"Thanks for the help last night."

"Not a problem. I can influence the creature, when it is in combat at least."

"Grok told me what happened. I thought we would have been in danger as well when you arrived."

"That is the common belief. I stay away from people because I can only influence the creature, not control it. You and Grok, as well as Zen, are safe. You are the ones who let me have that influence, because you are my friends. I sense you helping me when I fight the powers of the dark."

"Were you certain we were safe last night?"

"I have known for a long time. The first time I changed, I thought of Grok standing by me when other skrel had left. It stopped me from losing myself in the dark. I told Grok about it. The second time I changed, he was there the entire night. When I asked him why he had done something so dangerous, he told me that he trusted me." Leku glanced over to where Grok was asleep. "Is he?"

"He is not seriously hurt. Let him sleep for now."

With the fire now burning merrily, Thenk began to prepare food and *cwr.*

"Grok!" Leku nudged his friend.

"Hmm?"

"Time for breakfast."

Grok yawned and looked inquiringly at Leku. "I am well," the werewolf replied.

"Good. Thanks for last night."

After they had eaten Grok passed on his news.

"Those books we found yesterday? I cannot even tell what script they are in, but some pages have Tyranthian with the other script next to it. I think it might be a translation."

"So, someone could translate it," said Leku.

"Maybe. Calon Gan would know."

"Did you manage to understand any of the Tyranthian?" Thenk asked.

"Only a few words, nothing that will help us. We cannot wait for a translation, it could take weeks to do. The Spear is still out there somewhere. The books are in my pack, we will take them to Calon Gan."

"We have nothing left to do here. We should get going," said Thenk.

They were nearly at the road when Alron and his human companion stepped into their path. Grok and Leku recognised the human from the inn.

"In the name of the Council, stop!" said the elf.

"*Galth yn teryf, orc mand*," growled Grok, glaring at the elf.

The human began muttering as Alron spoke. "You must not interfere with our work. We have the Hammer Of Colwen, you will not take the Spear. You will be the first of the skrel to die."

The human sent a blast of energy at the skrel

before they could react. The red ray dissipated in front of Grok. He slowly walked forward, motioning the others to stay just behind him. Their assailants looked worried. The human cast another spell. A black ray ricocheted off nothing in front of Grok and hit the elf. He disappeared in a cloud of greasy smoke as the mage began to run. He did not get far before the skrel caught him.

"What do you want?" Grok said, firmly holding the human's shoulders.

"Why are you trying to kill us?" asked Leku.

"You are opposed to the Council! *Fint soirn joue.*" He vanished from Grok's grip.

"What just happened?" Thenk said.

"Some transport spell? He could be anywhere now," Leku replied.

"How did we survive that magic attack?" Thenk persisted.

"I have no idea. I thought no-one had that much magic ability."

The emergency teleport spell had removed the caster to a random point on the world. He achieved his goal and got away from the skrel, arriving on a mountain top thousands of miles from Beddcrul. He was congratulating himself on his escape when he heard a voice say, "I have been waiting for you." He turned to look at the cowled figure as the ground trembled. Seconds later, the volcano erupted.

Chapter IXX

When the skrel arrived back in Penmin, it was to the news that Grimevil had aligned itself with the Council.

"This is bad news indeed," said Calon Gan, when his guests were comfortable. "It means that events are moving faster than we had hoped. These books you recovered may be invaluable to us. They undoubtedly belonged to a mage guild. You see these defensive symbols on the covers?"

"Defensive symbols?" asked Thenk.

"Yes, capable of warding off any attack by magic, especially by a field of magic opposed to those of the writer."

"That is how we escaped then," said Leku. He told Gan what had happened as they left the ruins.

"I trust that mage is now far away. To be able to cast an annihilation spell in these times requires a considerable innate ability."

Magic had always been the province of a select few, either those who were born with the ability or those who spent many years studying it. A few magic users stayed outside the guilds but most joined, finding a guild that matched their interests and staying for life. Some individuals would use their abilities for free to help people but many would charge huge fees for spells. Rulers, nobles and rich merchants would employ a mage for assistance with their work or merely for an evening's entertainment. Each mage would pass on some of his money to his guild, which would take care of older mages and do charitable work.

Only in warfare was the use of magic banned, except when fighting demons. No guild was strong enough to stand against the rule until the Council came to power. The guilds knew of cycles in the amount of magic available, but they were unable to prevent the fading of magic which came after the Battle of the Plains of Harabrum. Most people were unaffected by the change; the stories they listened to were full of magic, but few had ever encountered it.

The mage guilds fell apart as the magic faded. Once rich, they fell into poverty as they were unable to charge for magic services. Their possessions were sold or taken and their buildings abandoned to the elements. Now only the Council could consider using magic beyond simple communication spells. When they connected to the Outer Darkness they would have access to its energy. That was what made them so dangerous.

The following day brought both good and bad news. There was word from travellers that a band of demons had attacked a village in Gamelen. The stories that survivors told spoke of mangled bodies spread around the streets as buildings burned.

The good news came in the person of Kerr Arguelen, a member of the Freidyn from Corbus. He was to help Calon Gan with research and would be able to translate the books found at Beddcrul. The skrel left the scholars alone and went out on the cliffs.

"Now we go to Monstrea," said Grok.

Leku grinned at Thenk. "Another sea voyage."

"Last night, I was looking at the maps the sailors use," Grok told them. "My grandfather's notes say that Monstrea is on the coast, but the maps do not show it."

"Would they show it?" Thenk asked.

"Those maps show towers, harbours, small villages. Everything along the coast is on there. Unless it is abandoned like Beddcrul, a place that people avoid and do not even talk about."

"We need to find out where it is."

Four figures were sitting at a table in the Skrelgrun Inn.

"It was demons?" Friy asked.

"Yes, the marks were unmistakeable. I have done what I can, but..." Pola tailed off.

"So near to town as well," Tola murmured.

"There were no signs of anything else?" Lok asked.

"Just some of their belongings around. It is like the old stories. The demons just come and go."

"It is just a warning of what will happen if the Council win," said Friy.

Grok and the others returned to Calon Gan's house by way of the market and arrived with provisions. Arguelen was already working on the books.

"Have the Freidyn any knowledge of Monstrea?" Thenk asked Calon Gan.

"It does exist but not on any charts. The ruins of Beddcrul have an unpleasant reputation. That of Monstrea is far worse. No one must know where you are going. I have nothing but written descriptions to help you find it. I hope that they will be enough."

"How do we get to the area?"

"By boat to the port of Afon. Then take the road to Brystan. The road stays close to the coast, but it turns inland to avoid Monstrea. I believe that it once ran through Monstrea, until the mages' village was abandoned. From that point, you will have to leave the road and search for the ruins. I believe that they are not easy to find."

"When can we go?"

"The next boat will leave tomorrow evening. You must be on it."

The Lonskat of Grimevil looked at the corpse in front of him, then turned to his guard captain.

"You did well, Schlaan. Any other agents of the Freidyn must be dealt with in the same way. Not only do they oppose our plans, they are allied with the monsters from the north. They say all can direct their rulers. How can many rule at once? That will be dealt with. Only those of limited intelligence believe that people can be trusted. Those of us who study history know that a single strong leader is needed to make a country great."

"Our people know of you as a great leader, Lonskat," Schlaan said, nervously. "They would never accept the teachings of monsters."

"You are loyal, Schlaan. You show good sense in ignoring the lies of the Skrel. You will be rewarded." He swept out of his office and headed for his private chambers, leaving the guard captain to relax.

Talking to the Lonskat was like playing with a

hungry bear, one mistake could be your last. Schlaan had learned to always suggest the people's strong support of the Lonskat and to criticise the skrel. The Lonskat had a deep-seated hatred of the northern race and feared them. His brother had been a member of Pure Land, he had travelled into the enemy's territory and killed many skrel. That crusading force were never heard of after their attack on a place called Tolgath. The loss of his brother had increased the Lonskat's hatred of the skrel and raised his brother to the status of the honoured dead. The skrel very rarely travelled as far south as Grimevil and had never interfered in the running of another country, yet the Lonskat suspected them of plotting against him. Any plots against him were by Grimevillians, the country's history of tyrants obtaining power by force meant that plots to overthrow the leader were commonplace.

The Lonskat was nearly at his quarters when his factotum came running up.

"Lonskat! We have had word from the head of the Geselftan. They believe they have a way to carry out your plan."

"Excellent. Then it is time to show the Council what we can do."

In the Tolgath longhouse, Zen was meditating. He sensed a darkness closing in on the world. A darkness with shapes moving in it. Shapes ready to enter the world, waiting for their time to come..

Amidst them was a larger shape. One who would terrify those other horrific shapes. A creature whose appearance could not even come from the tortured mind of a madman. Everything about it seemed wrong, its very shape an affront to the world. Those who had become aware of it had named it in the Ereinian tongue, *Carn ol Ochot,* Destroyer of Worlds. It sensed the presence of the skrel and rushed towards him.

"You never heard of *Carn ol Ochot?*" asked Grok.

"No," replied Leku.

"Nah," said Thenk.

The three skrel were outside an inn, enjoying some sunshine and beer.

"Probably too scary for kids. I know it from what my grandfather wrote and from Zen. Someone in Erein found it in the Darknesses and called it the Destroyer. There is a legend which says that it will appear at the end of the world. Compared to *Carn ol Ochot* those demons were like midges."

"Has it ever come through from the Darknesses?"

"Not that anyone knows of. The barriers keep it out. Apparently it does not have the power to push through. If they fell, it could come through, but no one would survive, some think that the world would not survive."

Silence fell again. After a short while, Thenk went for more beer. Leku turned to Grok. "You think this might not turn out well?"

"I do not think the Council really understand what could happen if they let the Xetal in and others from the Outer Darkness arrive. None of us could stand against them for long, they are far more powerful than the demons we fight against."

Chapter XX

The Inner Council was meeting in an underground chamber, worried about being observed by outsiders. They were discussing future plans.

"The leaders are to be destroyed. Kill the scholars but spare the priests," said Geoe. "The priests will be of use to us."

"Would the scholars have knowledge we can use?" asked Tonb.

"Some, but they ask questions. The priests teach people not to ask questions. For there to be peace and stability, we must have complete control. Not only the leaders and the scholars, but their families must be removed. The Freidyn must especially be destroyed forever!"

"The skrel?" asked another member.

"When we have secured our power, we will wipe out the skrel. Pure Land are correct in their beliefs about the skrel being an aberration on our world, an affront to all other living beings. Yet, they cannot remove the affront. The skrel will be gone from this world within a year of our victory."

"We can do that?" asked Chene.

"Yes, there is an ancient spell. Long forgotten by those outside this Council, but it will serve our purpose. We will solve the problem of the skrel, forever."

Geoe was silent while the councillors talked

amongst themselves.

"Remember that some people do not like the stability and peace we bring," he told the Councillors. "There are those who will say there is another way. They are dangerous people, when we find them they must be captured."

"And killed?"

"Not at first, Tonb. First we must learn all we can from them. You have ways of finding things out. Use them, then they die. Let their villages be razed and their neighbours put to death. All will see the results of opposing the peace and stability we bring."

Chapter XXI

The rain fell heavily as the skrel boarded the ship to take them to Afon. They had said goodbye to Gan at his house, and left the copper statue found at Beddcrul with him for safekeeping.

Low clouds hung like fog hung around the cliffs as the ship left her moorings. The crew muttered darkly that it was unnatural for the time of year. The swell was low, so that even Thenk was unaffected as they set sail. Once the ship was away from Penmin, the cook served up supper for the small number of passengers on board. Apart from the skrel, there were four humans and two elves. None looked suspicious. It was customary for the passengers to be sociable and spend time in polite discussion after the meal.

The elves spent a short time there before leaving.

Even Grok made an effort to be sociable and the evening passed pleasantly.

By the following morning the wind had freshened and the boat was rolling.

"I think I am going to die," Thenk moaned when Grok came to his bunk to ask how he was.

"That is the first part of seasickness."

"The second part is?"

"When you are afraid you are not going to die."

Leaving Thenk in peace, he went up on deck. The skies didn't look threatening but the winds were strong. Grok took some lungfuls of the fresh sea air and turned to look ahead of the bows, but his mind was already beyond the horizon. He knew nothing of Monstrea, yet he was thinking of it. Friy's words on the destruction of the Spear haunted him. The Council had the Hammer and they might not have learned of the Stone's destruction. They would be trying to find both artefacts. All three were needed to call the Xetal, yet Grok was worried. If he was in their position and learned that one was destroyed, he would find a way to use the two that still existed.

That evening the Lonskat was present at the building owned by the Geselftan. Their leader, a fussy, wizened old man, was bursting with excitement with news he had.

"This device, when given the correct energies, will be able to implement the plan you outlined to us."

The Lonskat looked at the contrivance of wheels, mirrors and brass arms melded together. The device was arranged in such a way that the mirrors could capture the energies flowing from the central glass-walled chamber. "Now, Hilner?

"Not yet, Lonskat. Unfortunately, the mineral it requires will not arrive for four days."

"Nothing else will do?"

"No, only this one mineral releases energy. When it arrives, we will place it into the machine, the energies will increase and then..."

"The barriers will fall!"

"For only a short time, Lonskat. We would require vastly more power to destroy them."

"A short time will be enough. Chaos will invade and the Council of Barakelth will see the power I can wield."

"They will see who the true leader is, Lonskat. You will return our land to its former glories."

"We will, Hilner. I chose well when I made you leader of the Geselftan. Yes, magic will return as in the old days and you will rank alongside your honoured ancestor as a Grimevillian hero and restore your family's name by erasing the shame of your father."

The sea was calm as the ship sailed into Afon. Thenk was still recovering from seasickness, so the skrel decided to set out the following morning. They had had little opportunity to plan on board the ship, so, when they had secured rooms for the night, they gathered in Grok's room and talked about what needed to be done.

"We have to get in, find the Spear and get out again," said Leku.

"The only way to deal with the Spear is to destroy

it. We need to get it back to Friy's forge," Thenk said.

"It will be difficult. We know that the Council has the Hammer of Colwen, they will be able to concentrate on the Spear if they know the Stone is destroyed. They might be able to cause trouble with just those two," said Grok. "We do not how they discovered which three they needed for the ritual. There may be an artefact they can use instead."

"We should pick up more provisions to avoid having to enter towns. We need to move overland fast."

Chapter XXII

The Council of Barakelth was meeting in the north of Grimevil.

"We know where the Spear of Pyra is ,Chene?"

"We think so, Tonb."

"Geoe is leading a party to Monstrea," said Terob.

"That is where it is hidden," the elf said. "When our leader returns in triumph, we will be ready. We have the hundred members of the Council, we will soon have the artefacts."

"We do not have the Stone of Erypmon," said Terob. "That was destroyed by the Skrel."

Chene's face darkened at the mention of the hated race. "They cannot defeat us so easily. Did you ever wonder how the Council came to use those three artefacts, Terob?"

"No."

"They spent much time searching for magical

artefacts of all kinds and testing them. The scholars of the Council spent their time testing them with their incantations. Those three artefacts, used together with the ritual of summoning, were the most powerful. The danger of one or more being destroyed was known. The Inner Council knew of other artefacts that would replace those destroyed. Those others were hidden before the Xetal were called, their purpose and location were kept by a few trusted Councillors. Those who survived the battle passed the knowledge to their children, the knowledge was kept alive and kept from our enemies.

"We have not merely been seeking the one hundred these past months. We have been finding the other artefacts. Some holders of the knowledge were not willing to part with it, until Tonb was able to persuade them otherwise. The Stone can be replaced and the ritual will be completed."

"The Xetal will once more be called."

"Then we will begin our work," said Tonb. "My instruments of persuasion are prepared. They have allowed us to find the artefacts and soon they will help us bring peace."

Terob glanced nervously at Tonb, the human wore a strangely contented expression when he talked of persuasion. Terob knew what methods were used and they scared him.

"Come, Terob," said Chene. "We have many things to talk of, elf to elf." She led the way into an open courtyard, where they could speak privately. "Your devotion to this Council is undying?" she asked.

"Yes, Chene."

"Your devotion to our glorious race, is that also strong?"

"Yes, Chene."

"Humans bring a certain interesting way of looking at matters. The inventiveness of Tonb in methods of persuasion has been most enlightening. They bring much to this Council, yet, it is the elves who will ultimately take control. We are the ones whose destiny is to lead. If your devotion to our people is as strong as you claim, you will be useful to me."

"Madam Chene, no one could ever say that anything can claim more devotion from me, than our race."

"Excellent, Terob. Come with me, we have work to do."

Chapter XXIII

Grok and the others split up to do the provisioning. Afon was a small town, most of the trade went through Brystan, along the coast, leaving Afon as the main fishing port. The people were friendly and curious about the skrel. There seemed to be no stories of demons or the Council, the townsfolk were more concerned with the state of the fishing. Having bought dried meat and fruits, together with other needed items, they met back at the inn, it was also quiet. They struck up a conversation with the innkeeper who had been looking anxiously out of the window.

"Yes, it is quiet tonight," he said in the inland dialect. "I do not like the look of those storm clouds."

The skrel looked at each other, concerned. "Bad weather?" rumbled Grok.

"Yes. Strange for this season. The weather has not been good this year." He paused. "What brings you to this part of the world?"

"We are looking for a man called Dylanth, he might be near Brystan," said Thenk.

"One of those travelling scholars?"

"Yes, he was asked to take care of a rare jewel. It was no longer safe in Grimevil, who would think a poor scholar would own such a jewel?"

"A scholar did pass through here some days ago. I do not know his name."

"We must find him soon. We have been told that the people searching for the jewel have discovered who is carrying it. If they reach him first, they will kill him. Our job is to protect him."

The innkeeper looked at them. "It would be a brave man who takes on all three of you."

The innkeeper was not surprised to see them leaving in the teeth of a gale along the Brystan road. He wished them well and told them that Dylanth would be welcome in his inn. It was an unpleasant journey in the wind. When the rain joined in it became worse.

Each skrel kept his thoughts to himself and Grok's were particularly dark. He could not shake the feeling that something very bad was approaching. Before long, things were going to change, possibly forever. He supposed he had known that ever since the decision was made by the Skrelton. But this seemed to be more serious. Decisions were what made life difficult. Dying was easy, everyone could do it. Living was the difficult thing. Being unsure whether the decisions one made were right made it even more so.

Less introspective than his friend, Thenk was occupied with the recovery of the Spear. He was fully aware of the potential for disaster, but he could put that aside to concentrate on the near future. What happened at Monstrea would determine what form the disaster would take, if there was one. When he knew what to expect, he would plan for it.

Leku knew more than the others of the darknesses and what lurked there. He alone knew what would break through should the Council call the Xetal. He was prepared to sacrifice himself to destroy the Spear if needs be, but for the moment he pushed that thought aside.

The light was fading fast and early as the road turned away from the coast. This was where they had to travel off the road.

"It is too late to look for Monstrea now," said Grok. "We need to find shelter for the night."

"If we stay on the road we should find something," Leku said. "Come on."

They walked along the Brystan road for some minutes before finding a small building. After no response to their knocking they opened the door and saw that no-one had lived there for some time. It was sound and warmed up after they made a fire. They took off their wet clothes and ate their first meal since breakfast at the inn. A simple meal of dried fruit and meat, followed by bread and cheese that the innkeeper had given them.

"Who was Pyra anyway?" asked Thenk, breaking the silence as they sat around the fire drinking *cwr.*

"I have something here," muttered Grok. He started hunting through his many pockets as the others waited. Eventually he found the parchment he was looking for.

"My grandfather's work,' he rumbled. He sighed as he realised he would have to read them the entire page.

"Pyra was human, a child when he was found washed up on the shores of Skrelbard after a shipwreck. A skrel family adopted him. It became obvious that he was a natural magic user. When he was old enough, he left Skrelbard to join the Cardiem Guild, known for their support of skrel mages. He rose quickly in the guild, but never forgot his home.

"At that time, the warlord Barteus ruled the northern shore of the mainland and eyed the forests of Skrelbard. His incursions were defeated, but skrel were killed defending their homeland. Pyra crafted a weapon for them, a spear of great power. It would kill instantly on striking and return to the hand of the fighter if it was thrown. Pyra knew that Barteus would try and capture the spear to use it against the skrel. Therefore, he imbued the weapon with magic that would destroy it forever if a skrel was killed by it.

"The Skrelton accepted the Spear from Pyra and Oden y Bralt used it at the next skirmish with the forces of Barteus. The warlord's fighters were routed. Oden allowed the survivors to return to Barteus, to tell him of the terrible spear and its power. When the warlord learned of the weapon and the warning that it could not be turned against the Skrel, he ceased his attacks on the island. Barteus was killed in a futile attempt to punish the Guild for treason, as it was in his lands. His youngest son became ruler and signed a treaty with Skrelbard. After many years of peace, the Skrelton returned the Spear to the Cardiem Guild for safekeeping.

"Generations later, with no skrel mages belonging to the Cardiem Guild, it joined the Council of Barakelth and the Spear passed into their hands," Grok finished.

Silence returned inside the building, the only noise coming from the howling gale outside. The wind remained severe all night and was still blowing strongly as they set off for the abandoned dwellings of Monstrea.

Once more, the Lonskat of Grimevil was visiting the Geselftan's building. Hilner, was rushing around his device in great excitement. The Lonskat looked at the small metal box that rested on the central chamber. "This is the mineral you have been waiting for?"

"Yes, Lonskat. This mineral is the key to the device."

"Begin."

Trembling with excitement the little man opened the box and took out a small rock with a pair of tongs. He placed it inside the central chamber of the device.

"The energy will build up now. When the chamber is full of light, it will be ready."

The Lonskat looked at the glass walled chamber

eagerly.   "Excellent."

Although he was trained in the more obscure arcane arts the Lonskat had very little understanding of the work carried out by the Geselftan. They had discovered ways to use natural elements which would mimic simple magic. This device would bring down the barriers. How and why did not bother him. The fact that they could was enough. All he knew and cared was that they could help to extend his rule beyond Grimevil's borders. With the Geselftan's help, he would restore the rightful place of Grimevil in the world.

The weather added to Grok's feeling of oppression as they crossed the rough country to the ruins of Monstrea. Leku was equally unsettled. He couldn't tell what it was, but something was starting to go terribly wrong in the world. There was a faint disturbance in the currents, as if the first breeze of a devastating storm had touched the land.

After they had walked for an hour or so, they began to see the stone walls. There were a number of still recognisable buildings among piles of rubble. Nature was reclaiming the site. Roads and trails were covered by grasses and shrubs.

"Where now?" asked Grok, looking around with dislike at the grey buildings. Even in a ruined state, he could see why the village had been avoided. A grey, sinister collection of buildings that must have loomed ominously over nearby travellers without any lighted windows to cheer the scene. The windows perpetually dark, adding to the brooding presence of the abandoned buildings. Even in bright sunshine it must have been ominous. So, the road was abandoned and travellers formed a new route, away from Monstrea. Grok shivered as he looked up at a round building, the smooth grey walls stretching unbroken to the ring of dark windows at the top. It did not look chilling, yet it radiated malevolence.

"The sooner we can leave here, the better," he said.

Leku glanced at him. "You are not normally worried by buildings."

"There is something wrong here. Maybe just a trace of the past, but I do not like it."

"The main building was probably in the centre," said Thenk. "They used to build cellars and passages underground. I have learned some things when I'm travelling," he added when they looked at him. "Storage and ways to get out of the building when you did not want to be seen coming and going, especially near the coast."

A fast survey showed which building they needed. It was roofless and part of one wall had collapsed. Grok reluctantly walked inside, the feelings he had about the buildings were worse in here. It seemed to have been a central hall. Stone fireplaces were set along the walls and old tables and chairs could still be seen. In one corner, Thenk found a flagstone with a rusted iron ring set into it. He pulled on the ring and the stone rotated upwards on a hinge, revealing a dark pit. Grok took a couple of torches from his pack and his flint and tinder from a pocket.

"Someone should stay here," Leku said as Grok lit the torches.

The others nodded. "If we find another entrance, we can come back for the guard," said Grok. "I would be happier if we had another way out."

A brief round of rock-cloth-axe settled that Leku would be the guard. Thenk threw a torch down the hole and saw handholds in the stone as the light dropped. He climbed down and caught the other torch Grok threw him before climbing down himself.

The passageway smelled musty but the torches burned bright and clean as they cautiously moved along. The walls were made of stone blocks with occasional empty torch brackets.

Thenk felt a slight movement under his foot as they walked, and cried "Look out!"

Not knowing what would happen, they dropped to the floor. Then Grok leapt forward as he saw a stone door descending to block the corridor. Throwing the torch underneath it, he got his shoulder under the slab. He was able to slow the descent as Thenk crawled underneath. Then he was able to pull himself through. The door settled onto the floor a few inches from his boot.

They saw two other traps on their route that had been sprung years ago. At the third trap, the skeletons of a human and an elf were pinned to the wall with steel bolts. After ten minutes of walking, they came to a T-shaped junction. A faint whiff of sea air came to them from the left while blackness stretched off to the right.

They walked down the right-hand way just far enough to see that it contained enough doors to be worth searching before turning back. A short way along, it began to get lighter and they saw stone steps leading up. They led up to an entrance concealed among the hillocks. The remains of a wooden trapdoor lay nearby. Presumably it had concealed the entrance once.

Looking around carefully to make sure that there was no one present, Grok climbed out of the hole and found himself near the edge of the cliff a short way from Monstrea. Unseen in the heavy rain, the sea crashed against rocks far below. He leaned down to speak to Thenk. "Our other way out. You wait there while I get Leku. If you hear a wolf howling, it means we cannot find this hole." He ran back in the direction of the grey ruins.

His eyes barely above the surrounding hillocks, Thenk kept watch for any enemies. He saw no signs of anyone until Leku and Grok came into view. As they neared, he saw them looking around and heard a low howl. He stood up so that they could see him and ducked back down. Checking there were no observers, the skrel let themselves into the hole and walked down the passage.

In Monstrea, a group of people was waiting. Elves and humans from different lands but all in fine clothing.

Their leader turned to them. "We believe that the Spear of Pyra is here. We are sure that the Skrel are searching for it. We must find it before they do. Move!"

They fanned out, searching for any sign of where the Spear might be.

The skrel had examined several rooms. They had located a number of possibly magical items but no Spear. They took nothing, since it would take an experienced mage to safely clear the area. Random magical objects are inherently dangerous and needed training to safely deal with. There were few enough with the skills these days so magic items tended to be dumped unless they were well understood.

All three were tense. There was a faint magical field due to the items but it seemed to be growing stronger somehow. Even away from the buildings, Grok felt uncomfortable. Leku became aware of dark forces beginning to stir.

The werewolf slowly opened another door and Grok's axe swung up and down in the opening. When no traps were activated, Leku carefully stepped through. The room seemed to have been used as a store. A number of boxes and barrels stood around. It did not look hopeful, then he spotted a long thin box hidden away in a corner.

Moving gingerly, he crossed to the box and opened it. It opened easily to reveal a spear. The others came across when he called and looked at it. Grok pointed at a carved word.

"I've seen that in my grandfather's writings. It's an old spelling of Pyra."

"The Spear of Pyra just lying here?" asked Thenk.

"Who would think to look for a major artefact in a storeroom?" Leku asked. "They probably never imagined the place would be deserted like this. Maybe the person who hid it intended it to be here for a short time. Whoever they were, they never came back for it."

"Then, when they abandoned the guild, no one knew it was here."

"Yeah, now we have to get out of here," said Grok.

They hustled back down the corridor, heading for the entrance by the cliffs. Thenk was the last to climb up and heard the noise of shouting on the lines of "Stop them!" from the passageway behind him.

"Run!" he shouted, as he pulled himself up.

The rain had thickened into a coastal fog with the lessening of the wind. They ran into it, relying on memory to guide them inland. Leku risked a glance back and saw a couple of elves readying bows. The arrows missed their targets, thudding into the ground to the right of the skrel. The ground was uneven and in the fog they couldn't navigate easily, but they had to keep moving. No one else would realise what the Spear was and they had to keep it away from the Council.

Eventually they slowed to a walk. Unable to tell if the Council were tracking them, they kept moving. They had no idea how far inland the fog stretched but they would have to navigate once it cleared, wherever they were. The sound of the sea had faded, so they were further from the cliffs at least. They paused when they neared a small stone building.

"We need a plan," said Thenk. "We can hide there while we work out what to do. If they are following us we might not have much time but it is the best we have."

As they approached the building they heard the

noise of hoofbeats and an elf rider appeared through the fog.

"I can smell the stench of skrel from a mile off!" he shouted, swinging his rapier. Thenk ducked under the blade as Grok's axe slashed the elf's leg. Leku growled at the horse which took fright. Whilst the elf struggled to control his horse, Thenk struck with the weapon he was carrying, the Spear. The elf's flesh turned to ashes and blew off the bones, leaving a skeleton to be carried off by the panicking horse.

"Inside!" shouted Thenk.

They ran to the door and barricaded it behind them. The building was well fortified and stocked with weapons. Grok examined some of the bows on the wall, the bowstrings were old and not maintained. The draw was less than he liked, but they would do.

"What now?" asked Thenk, he was still shocked by the way the Spear had killed the elf.

"If the rest of those *kreltarn* stay away we keep going," said Grok. "We need to find a port and a ship we can sail to Skrelbard. Friy must destroy the Spear as soon as he can."

"If they do come, we can stay here for some time," Leku said. "The walls and the door are to strong to break down easily."

It was not long before the Council did appear. One of the humans appeared to be staring into space. He was using a little understood talent to look a short way into the past.

"The building there, they are in there!" His eyes refocused and he sagged, worn out from the effort.

Some of the humans moved in to attack the door

but it had been strongly built. Grok and Thenk fired some arrows out of the narrow slits in the walls. The arrows deterred the Council and they withdrew a short way.

"The door is too strong, Leader Geoe," said a human. "The skrel can shoot at us from cover."

"The door is strong, but wood is not resistant to fire. Listen to me," said Geoe.

Inside, the skrel discussed their options.

"They cannot get at us here but we cannot get out," said Grok.

"We just need one of us to get away with the Spear," Thenk said.

"If there is another door, I cannot find it," said Leku. " The only other way out is through that trapdoor and onto the roof. We could get out there and climb down, but that would be dangerous."

"Dangerous," murmured Thenk. "Do you remember what Friy said?"

Grok thought. "No," he growled.

"Yes! You can call Death and get us back."

"Only if he keeps his word. We cannot rely on that."

"Grok. If the Council get the Spear now, not only will we die but Skrelbard will be in danger. One skrel life against the lives of all Skrel. I do not want to die. But if that is what it takes to save everyone in Tolgath, I will."

"Thenk is right," said Leku. "One of us has to be sacrificed to save the rest. If Death does not bring him back then so be it. I have faced death, it does not scare me. What scares you is killing a friend. You fought Death and defeated him. You have the power to end this if you have the strength."

"Listen to Leku, you are the one. I cannot do it myself, I would not have the reach. Someone needs to use the Spear."

"You just calmly expect me to put a spear through your heart?" Grok growled.

"No, I am not calmly doing anything. I do not want to be here saying this! But we are here and I am scared about what will happen. But what I do know is that we have no choice if we want to save our friends and families on Skrelbard!"

"So someone else I care about has to die for other people's actions! Leku is right. Some things you cannot ask a skrel to do!"

"So, the world will end and you did not prevent it because you were too weak!"

Leaving the two arguing, Leku went to investigate a faint smell. He reached the source at the door. Outside, the Council had piled some torches by the door and doused the whole thing with oil. A spark did the rest.

Grok and Thenk's glaring contest was interrupted by Leku. "They are burning down the door," the werewolf told them.

"You must do it!" shouted Thenk.

"I cannot kill either of you!"

"We will come back."

"You trust Death that much?" Grok snarled.

"We have no choice! You are the only who can call Death and Leku cannot kill us."

"You must," Leku broke in. "One of us or all of us. Then how many others after the Council comes to power?"

"It is the only thing you can do," Thenk told Grok, gently.

From a corner, the cowled figure watched with interest.

Grok turned away from them, his nails digging into his hands, muscles tense. Leku could scent the tension coming off him. He stood there a full minute, his breathing fast and shallow.

"Th....Thenk. It has to be...you...Leku will not let me bring him....back," Grok said, his voice low and shaking.

Thenk nodded and began to remove his coat and shirt. As he did so he whispered to Leku, "If this does not work, tell Elea what happened."

Leku looked at him, Thenk was calm now, the decision accepted, "I will not need to."

Grok did not turn around until Leku told him they were ready. His friends were shocked by the expression of pain on his face. He could not speak and held out a shaking hand for the Spear. As Leku handed it to him, he saw that Grok's hands were covered in blood, his nails had cut into his flesh. Grok was sweating, every part of his mind bar one screaming at him not to do this.

Leku put a hand on his shoulder, "You must. Then call Death."

Barely able to see, Grok aimed the Spear. His eyes met Thenk's and he thrust the Spear forward.

The last thing Thenk heard was Grok's voice roaring, "DEATH!"

Chapter XXIV

Death stepped forward from his corner and looked at the two skrel on the ground. Grok had collapsed as the Spear turned to dust in his hands.

"You expect me to uphold our agreement?" Death asked.

"Yes!"

Death was silent.

"You will," growled Grok

Death did not respond. From his position on the floor, Grok leapt at him, looking so savage that Death took a step back.

"You are serious, that is what you had to prove. I am not malicious and I keep my word. Your friend does not deserve to die here and now for his bravery in defending your world. Look."

The wound in Thenk's chest closed up. The colour returned to his face and he began to breathe.

"Our agreement is completed," Death said as he stepped back into the corner. "I am taking a day away from my post. None of you can die until the sun has set." He faded away.

"It worked," said Thenk, sounding surprised. "What now?"

"Get ready to leave," muttered Grok, opening his pack.

Leku crossed to Thenk and examined him. "You smell normal," the werewolf said. "It is going to take Grok some time to recover. Just do not mention this."

He was happy with Thenk's condition and moved to where Grok was taking bandages out of his pack.

He took a bandage off Grok and began to dress his friend's hands as Thenk dressed. The scents of stress were fading from Grok, but there was a hint of something else.

When they were ready, Leku stood on Thenk's shoulders and pushed open the trapdoor. He climbed up onto the roof and caught the rope Thenk threw to him. The trapdoor had a heavy iron ring set into it. Leku tied the rope to the ring and stood on the trapdoor as the others climbed up. He looked at the bandages on Grok's hands as his friend climbed out. Some blood was seeping through, but he knew he would not be allowed to help any more.

"I think they are all watching the fire," Thenk whispered. "Death said we cannot die. So we get out of here as fast as possible."

They dropped the rope down the wall opposite the door and quietly climbed down. When they were all on the ground they ran in the general direction of the road. Any slight noise they made must have been deadened by the fog. As they ran they heard the noise of axes on wood coming from the building. They slowed down as they approached the Brystan road, heading north. The fog was thinner and they could hear no signs of pursuit. They paused to drink from their water bottles and continued walking towards Brystan.

"It is time Lonskat," said Hilner. "The device is ready."

"At last." The Lonskat pulled the switch, for a moment there was response. Then they felt as the very air had shuddered at what was happening. Through the lands children started to cry. Men wondered where their weapons were and women rushed to secure their homes. A feeling of foreboding settled over everyone.

Leku was the first to feel it. "The barriers are down," he told the others. They did not question him but prepared their weapons.

"How?" asked Thenk.

"I do not know, but it feels as if Skrelbard is safe. Something else has happened."

"When is sunset?" Thenk asked.

Grok, still looking strained, replied. "We have a few hours yet."

"We need to find shelter. Come on."

They continued up the road at a faster pace, watching all the time, wondering if demons would suddenly attack.

At his home Calon Gan picked up a small toy. It was a magical cube that would show different pictures. The underlying level of magic was so low that it could take minutes to change. As he looked at it changed, then again and again.

It took him a moment to realise what he was seeing. Then he ran for the communication device in the corner. Abandoned by the Freidyn due to the lack of magic, it might now be working.

The members of the Council of Barakelth that were gathered in Grimevil looked at each other, realising what was happening.

"The barriers are down!" said Terob.

"Tonb, Terob, come with me," said Chene. They followed her to a separate room. "This effect may not last long but it is our chance. The Stone of Erypmon has been destroyed by our enemies, but with the level of magic this high we can use another artefact. The Ring of Chouin is here. I can cast a spell that will give it the power to go beyond this world. It was made to transport the wearer anywhere in the known lands. I will make travel to the Outer Darkness."

"That will succeed?" asked Terob.

"Yes, for one time only. The Stone of Erypmon opened a portal from this world. The Ring will take the Spear and the Hammer into the Outer Darkness and open the portal there. The artefacts will be forever lost in the Darkness, but the portal will be open. We will have won!"

All through the lands demons appeared and began to attack. The combat was unplanned and disorganised, random attacks before the demons vanished again. The skrel travellers found the results of one attack at a farmhouse near the Brystan road. The human family had been killed and the terrified livestock were only now calming down. A black and white dog slunk up to Grok and whined softly, looking for his protection. He let it sniff his hand and scratched it behind the ears as he spoke to the others. "You want to stay here?"

"It is as good as anywhere," said Thenk. "If anyone survived, we can help them."

Leku nodded in agreement.

A brief search revealed no sign of living humans and their shouts were not answered. The inside of the farmhouse was empty of bodies, so they fastened the doors and windows to prevent demons getting in. The dog, looking a bit brighter, stuck close to Grok.

Night fell as they made supper from the supplies in their packs, though Grok let the dog have most of his share. There was little conversation and after they had finished eating, Thenk stood up.

"I am going to rest for a while," he said. "Can you two keep a watch till I get back?"

"Yes," Grok rumbled.

"Go and rest," Leku told him.

Thenk let himself into one of the rooms in the back of the house and lay on the bed. He was aware that its former owner was lying dead outside. But his own emotions were in turmoil after the events of the day and he could not be that worried about a stranger who was now beyond all aid.

Left alone in the kitchen Leku, Grok and the dog sat in silence in front of the fire. The dog crossed to a bowl of water for a drink. Then he moved to Leku for an ear scratch, before walking back to his protector.

Leku stood up. "They could come at us from either side. I will watch the back," he said.

Grok nodded. As Leku left the room, holding one of their candles, he heard a faintly growled "Thanks."

The dog rested his chin on Grok's knee and looked at him with the trust that only dogs have. Grok looked down at him and stroked his head.

"You are lucky dog. You just need someone to look

after you. You have no concerns about big questions."

The dog curled up at Grok's feet and sighed happily, knowing there was a friend with him. Grok looked into the fire. "Are we lucky or cursed to be intelligent?" he asked the dog. "To have to make decisions and live with them. Knowing that there are other ways things could have happened. Memory can be a burden. You just have simple things to remember, me, I remember more. Things that needed to be done and things that I was not there to prevent. All the time being aware that there must have been some way to prevent it happening. Even if omnipotence was the only way, why couldn't you have been omnipotent for that moment?

"If you are alive, you suffer. I heard of a group that claims suffering will lead to great rewards after death. What a way to keep oppressed people happy with their terrible lives. For those of us in the real world, life attacks from all angles and finally kills you. At the same time, there are always things that make it worthwhile." He looked down at the dog. "Krarg would have liked you, he always loved dogs."

Thenk awoke from a doze and saw a shape by the window. "Leku? What are you doing?"

"Guarding," Leku replied.

"Where is...?"

"Grok has the front, he is in the kitchen. He needs to be alone. The only skrel who can help him deal with what happened today, is Grok."

"But I am alive."

"Yes, but Grok did kill you. Not some demon or

other enemy threatening his life. He killed his friend, even though he knew you could come back," He paused. "If Death had not honoured his agreement Grok would have destroyed him. If we win this fight against the Council then Grok will know that you died for a reason, that will help him. Until that time, he will be unsure that your death had any meaning."

"You are sure he will get over this?"

"Not all werewolves can resist the dark pull, those that give in are highly dangerous. A werewolf I called a friend succumbed. I had to kill her."

Chapter XXV

The morning that dawned was clear and bright, the sort of morning that makes people feel that all is right with the world, regardless of the known facts. The dog was stretched out by the dying fire as Grok woke up, feeling stiff from sleeping in the chair. After checking that there were no demons around he went out to the yard. Dousing himself with water from the pump cleared his head but did nothing for his muscles. He pulled the bandages off his hands as he walked back into the kitchen. Leku was there preparing food, watched by the dog.

The werewolf looked up as he heard Grok. "There is some of Pola's salve on the table. Put it on your hands."

Grok gave him a look, but picked up the small pot. "How is Thenk?" he asked, as he smeared the aromatic cream on his palms.

"He is perfectly healthy. You need fresh bandages."

"We need to leave soon."

"We eat, then leave. The barriers are rebuilding."

"Are you sure?"

"They are stronger than they were last night. But I have no thoughts as to why they collapsed."

"Hey!" came Thenk's voice. Grok and Leku turned to see him standing in the doorway that led to the rest of the house.

"How are you feeling?" Grok asked.

"Hungry. What do we have for for breakfast?"

The morning dawned clear in Skrelbard, as the inhabitants took stock of a night without the barriers. There were some casualties. Many more were injured as they fought off the demons that had appeared.

Tolgath had been attacked, Pola was busy treating wounds and sending younger skrel out to gather more plants. Zen had discovered that an old magical mirror had begun to work again. His first experiment with it was to send a message to Calon Gan asking for news. The connection was poor, but they were able to speak to each other.

"I cannot tell what happened to the barriers," said Calon Gan. "The Freidyn have no records of such a collapse ever happening."

"Neither do we," Zen replied. "I fear some new evil is in the lands. What news of our travellers?"

"They have gone to Monstrea. What they seek was not in Beddcrul, I do not expect them to return for several days."

" I have discovered a new danger, Carn ol Ochot is aware of us. If the gateway is opened for the Xetal, he may come through. The Outer Darkness is infinite, we must hope that he is far away from the gateway. He could pass through if he is near it."

"If he does, none of us have the power to stop him," said Calon Gan.

"Yes, the Council must be stopped before they open a portal."

"We must wait now to hear from the travellers. They may have solved that issue for us."

"The rain may fall out of sight, but the river will pass your door. We have to trust in their abilities."

The members of the inner Council were meeting in Grimevil.

"I received a message from the Lonskat," said Geoe. "He states that he is the one who brought down the barriers."

"Do you believe him, Geoe?"

"I do, Tonb. He has unknowingly assisted us by increasing the level of magic drastically. That enabled my group to transport ourselves from Monstrea in an instant. Chene has cast the appropriate spells over the Ring of Chouin. Also, we have this." He opened a small pouch and tipped dust on to the table in front of him. "We searched for magic in the building where the skrel hid and found this."

"What is it?" asked Terob.

"All that remains of the Spear of Pyra."

"How could those bestial skrel destroy such an artefact?" Chene asked, her voice trembling with anger.

"I do not know," Geoe replied. "With this dust, we can increase the power of Skallag's Bane. That will be our third artefact. Skallag's Bane will still require its sacrifice though."

"Who would be the sacrifice?" Chene asked.

"We have a candidate, Chene. The Lonskat is ambitious. Our first objective requires him for our attack on Corbus. He must be the one to order his forces to attack. Later, we can perform the ritual of summoning and call the Xetal. Then Skallag's Bane will be free to take its sacrifice."

"Excellent."

"Now, call the full Council and our followers. I must speak to them."

The skrel were making good time to Brystan. A lightly loaded cart had passed them on the road and given them a ride, the black and white dog still with Grok. Brystan, an inland town, was connected to the sea by a navigable tidal river. Thenk, taking advantage of the general worry, was able to persuade the captain of a Penmin-bound ship to move his departure to the current high tide.

"We have news of great importance for a learned man there," he said, waving the parchment the Skrelton had given him.

"Will this news stop more attacks by demons?" the captain asked.

"It will." Thenk told him.

"Lads, we sail before noon!" The captain told his crew, as the skrel prepared for the journey.

Geoe looked at the Council members and others in front of him. He recognised the Lonskat of Grimevil and an older man in white seated next to the Grimevillian leader. He cleared his throat, it was time to speak.

"My fellow councillors, friends. We are nearing our great day. The Council of Barakelth has risen from its ashes and is strong again. Our friend, the Lonskat of Grimevil, has allowed us to prepare for the opening of the Way. Once that has been achieved, we shall take back what was ours. For too long now there has been fighting between peoples of the same land. Too many have died for petty squabbles. This is the time for the Council to step forward and do our duty. We shall bring peace and stability to these lands.

"But we must fight to do so! There are those who do not wish to see stability. They must be defeated! We will first move on the lands of Tildeth and Corbus. When we have secured the area of Barakelth we will be unstoppable. The Xetal will be with us and we will forge ahead, even unto the shores of Skrelbard! Peace shall reign under the rule of the Council!"

The listeners stood as one and applauded.

"We will all have our part to play in the approaching endeavour," Geoe continued. "Do not let any of you think you are less worthy to fight than others. The light of our peaceful rule will spread over the lands now wreathed in shadows. We all bear the torch of the future, a future of peace and prosperity. A future where humans and elves can live in the knowledge that there will be no further attacks by those races that would oppose us!"

After many speeches had been made and the Councillors were mingling with their supporters, the man in white spoke to Geoe.

"Leader Geoe. I am Teldarn, the leader of the Caran Church. We pledge our loyalty to you. There are many who do not accept the Word. Then there are the heathens of Skrelbard. They must all be dealt with."

"Thank you, Teldarn. With your help we will bring truth as well as stability to the land. With our help, you will be able to spread the Word. As with those who oppose the peace we bring, those who oppose your Truth will suffer."

Chapter XXVI

It was late in the evening when the skrel came to Penmin. Southerly winds had allowed them to make good time travelling along the coast, they had arrived a day earlier than they expected. When Calon Gan answered the knock at his door he noticed that Grok was looking worn, but the others seemed in good health.

"What news my friends?" he asked.

"The Spear of Pyra is destroyed," Thenk answered. "We do not know any reason for the barriers to fail."

"Neither do we. I fear some new evil from the Council. Come in, come in."

Calon Gan bustled round, putting a kettle on for

cwr, as the skrel set down their packs. "I have been speaking to Zen," he continued. "The level of magic has been raised by the fall of the barriers. There were some demons in Skrelbard, but Zen said that there was nothing for you to be concerned with."

He went out to the kitchen to continue making the *cwr*. The skrel looked at each other.

"Either there is nothing wrong in Tolgath, or people have been hurt and he does not want us to worry," Grok said. "We have to trust what he says."

The others nodded as Gan returned. "I have been researching something," he said. "Arguelen mentioned an old reference which reminded me of something I heard once. He has returned to Alghol with the books. There was a story regarding a weapon that was created to destroy the Council during the last war. It was to be used as a last resort, created by a powerful mage. The weapon was prepared but never used after the success on the Plains of Harabrum. The mage died without revealing the location himself. Though it is possible that others knew and made a record of the location."

"Will it still work?" Thenk asked.

"If the stories are correct, it is an extremely magical artefact that time will not affect. I can think of reason for it to be ineffective now. I have been searching through some old writings and I believe that I am close to discovering the location. If you can wait until my work is finished we will travel together and find the artefact."

It was later still, after Calon Gan had retired, that Thenk stepped outside. Grok was standing there staring out to sea, the half moon shining on him.

"Hey," said Thenk.

Grok did not reply but Thenk saw an expression of acknowledgement cross his face. Used to his friend's taciturnity he continued. "About destroying the Spear."

"We found a new way to do it," Grok told him.

"But Friy said..."

"You know what happened, so do Leku and myself. Some might guess. For the rest, what happened never happened. We found a new way."

Thenk took a moment to follow Grok's speech. "If you say so. All I have to say, is that I would not have trusted anyone else to do what you did."

Calon Gan continued his research the following day. He was surrounded by old manuscripts and parchments, some in strange languages. Leku and Thenk headed into Penmin to search for supplies for the upcoming journey. Grok set off along the cliffs with the black and white dog, whom he had named Zehc. They were on a circular walk that would take them along the coast, then inland and back to Penmin.

There was a fresh breeze blowing off the sea bringing the smell of salt up on the cliffs. Grok paused to look over the ocean as Zehc chased after a rabbit. What lay over there? Strange lands, strange people. He had heard that trolls lived over the sea, as well as dark furred intelligent apes. He turned around to look at the moorland behind him, covered in gorse and heather. If he had too, he could live there. It was not Skrelbard but it would do. The sea breeze kept the temperature cool as the sun rose higher and he continued along the cliffs.

Thenk and Leku had taken lunch at a tavern in Penmin and were carrying their supplies up the hill, when they saw Calon Gan hurrying towards them.

"I have it!" he called. "Follow me!" With a speed surprising for his age, he raced back up the hill. The skrel ran after him to his house.

"It was so obvious!" Calon Gan shouted, crossing to his desk. "We are looking for the Pyramid of Khelton Leveth! We are the only ones who know its location now. It is located in the most obvious place, at Barakelth! The Council must travel to their original seat of power, it is only there that they can fully control their magic. We must go there and find the Pyramid, before they can take control."

"How can we use it?" asked Leku.

"The records say that there is an inscription on the Pyramid itself. The words must be spoken to activate the Pyramid. We must leave as soon as possible, where is Grok?"

"Wandering somewhere," Leku replied.

"We will prepare now and leave first thing," said Calon Gan.

Grok and Zehc walked in as they were working. "Are we travelling again?" asked Grok.

"We are leaving in the morning," Thenk told him.

" For where?"

"Barakelth. To destroy the Council."

Chapter XXVII

The full Council had met once more. In a cave, the one hundred members had gathered to perform a rite. The Hammer of Colwen lay in pride of place.

Geoe held up a silver ring. "The Stone of Erypmon has been destroyed by our enemies. This is the Ring of Chouin, it will serve in the stead of the Stone. The Spear of Pyra has been destroyed. Here I have its remains with Skallag's Bane. Where is the blood sacrifice for Skallag?"

An ox was dragged towards him. Dabbing it with oil he began to perform the rite.

"*Elcon renda un pace,*" he intoned.

"*Un pace deteum parla,*" the Councillors replied.

"*Aras teum de nonus, cave non erat lare meum. Artus quo amas bracha uras chordan, tarandanus el pace un carla*" Geoe chanted as he picked up a curved silver knife and cut the ox's throat. The blood was collected in a copper bowl, which Geoe placed on an altar behind him, still chanting. The sword, Skallag's Bane, began to glow. Geoe dropped some of the Spear of Pyra's dust onto it, the rest into the bowl of blood. The glowing sword became brighter as the Councillors continued to chant.

"*Alces, trigem quo pace!*" shouted Geoe, as the sword's glow brightened suddenly then dimmed.

As the glow faded, so did their chanting. All three artefacts lay on the altar with the copper bowl, now empty of blood. Geoe turned and spoke to the Council. "We now prepare for the Rite of Zetron. All of us will travel to the site of Ottaran in Corbus. It is there we will call the Xetal, and take our next step to regaining power!"

Calon Gan managed to contact Zen before the group left Penmin, the level of magic was beginning to fade and contact was difficult..

"The artefact has been destroyed!" Calon Gan shouted.

"Good," said Zen's voice, faintly. "How are the travellers?"

"They are well! We are travelling once more. It is not safe to tell you our destination."

"I understand. There may be others listening. There are more..." Zen's voice faded as the spell failed.

"I hope he had nothing of importance to tell us," said Thenk.

Grok had made arrangements for Zehc to be taken care of in Penmin. He left the dog with a friend of Calon Gan's, together with some food and a carved stick that Zehc enjoyed playing with. Calon Gan and the skrel left Penmin under threatening clouds, they had hired a cart and two equoths for the journey. Barakelth was near the border of Erein and Corbus and there was no time to make the journey on foot.

In his mansion, the Lonskat of Grimevil relaxed as he waited for the top general of his army to arrive. He had ordered all those able to enchant weapons and armour to work until the magic had faded. The enchantments would hold for some time after. He glanced at the closed door. "Come in, General!"

There was a pause and the door opened to admit General Gracus. As always when the Lonskat answered the door before before anyone knocked, he looked mildly confused. The same as all leaders who obtain and maintain their position by force, the Lonskat was dominated by paranoia. Simple spells alerted him whenever his rooms were approached and identified the person.

"Your orders, Lonskat?" the General asked, recovering his poise.

"Your orders are simple, General. Attack Corbus and Eltylon immediately."

"Yes sir."

Gracus withdrew and the Lonskat smiled to himself. This was just the start. Soon he would wrest control from the Council and be the ultimate ruler. His mind teetered on the brink and drifted back to sanity, but before long it would have to fall.

The Lonskat had long planned his attacks and the lands of Corbus and Eltylon were swiftly invaded. Their leaders, whilst nervous after recent events, had not anticipated a full-scale invasion. The forces near the border with Grimevil were not capable of resisting for long.

Chapter XXVIII

Hauk stretched and got up from his position by the fire to circle the campsite. All quiet. The other skrel were asleep as he sat down to continue his watch. They did not know all the details but enough to worry them. They knew that Thenk had been sent south to search for the Spear and the Hammer but nothing else. These skrel were a group who had decided that skrel help would be needed if the Xetal came through. They were headed for southern Corbus, where the ruler lived.

Tharn of Tolgath had spoken of Thenk being assisted by one of his fellow villagers and a human. He had also mentioned that at least one of the Tolgath Skrelton supported their plan. "Whilst old skrel sit and talk, young skrel do what we talk about," Zen had said. Tharn had not told his companions that Leku was also with Grok and Thenk. He had met Leku and liked the werewolf, but even the Skrel could have odd ideas about shapeshifters.

It was later that day that Tharn, Hauk and the others were walking along a road. They had left their equoths at a village some time ago when the animals were obviously too tired to continue. The equoths had been in poor shape when the skrel had bought them and now had owners who would care for them.

They heard a cart approaching them. Hauk was turning to flag down the cart in hopes of a ride, when he was hailed in Skrellian. They all turned to see a skrel driving the cart. He reined in the equoths and scanned the group.

"Tharn! What are you doing so far from Tolgath?"

"Thenk!" Tharn exclaimed. He briefly explained why they were there as the other riders on the cart climbed down to meet them.

"What did Zen think?" rumbled Grok.

"He agreed with the idea."

"That is good and bad," growled Grok. The others looked at him inquiringly. "You are doing something good, but he thinks something bad is going to happen."

He refused to be drawn more on the matter and the other skrel climbed on the cart. Thenk again acted as driver and the equoths pulled the cart down the road.

The Council had travelled into Corbus and were camped at an ancient site. They had begun the journey to Barakelth, but now was the time and place to summon their allies. The area was prepared; the Ring of Chouin, Skallag's Bane and the Hammer of Colwen were in place. They rested on top of a large smooth stone. The sheer granite walls on three sides would reflect and focus the energies formed.

The full Council was present, formed into a semicircle facing the artefacts. Geoe was in the centre, Tonb and Chene either side of him. He raised his voice in a chant that had not been heard since the Council last held power. The echoes bounced off the granite as the other Councillors began to chant along. A simple rhythmic chant that focused the minds of the chanters. Thought faded and rhythm became dominant.

As the chant continued, the artefacts began to draw power from the Councillors. Energy leached from the rocks as atoms decayed. The artefacts glowed with a strange yellow light and faded from view. A small pinpoint of light appeared above the stone they had rested on. Slowly, it grew until it was three feet in diameter. Then a black dot appeared in the centre and began to grow. It expanded until it was a wide black circle surrounded by a thin white ring.

A vague, formless shape appeared in the circle and passed through it. Hard to see in the air, it moved aimlessly before purposefully travelling to a Councillor. The shape faded from view and the woman's eyes glazed as she spoke. "We are the Xetal." She looked around the group. "Who speaks for you?"

Geoe walked forward. "I am the leader of the Council of Barakelth."

"Why do you call us?"

"Long ago, the Council and the Xetal joined forces. We were defeated by the actions of our enemies, but now we are strong enough to once more take control of these lands."

"You wish our help?"

"We do. This land can only be stable and peaceful when it is under the rule of this Council. That is our aim!"

"What will become of us when you have your victory?" the Xetal asked.

"You will have what you wish," Geoe told it.

"What we wish," the Xetal said softly. "There will be battles?"

"There will."

"Then we accept. It will take time for us to travel here. But call for us when you are ready."

The Councillor's face relaxed and she crumpled to the ground. Her neighbours bent to look at her as Geoe spoke to the entire Council. "You have heard the word of the Xetal! We will be victorious!"

Chapter IXXX

The Skrel continued their journey and reached a village called Kelrith, there they stopped. They had not intended to stop but the road was blocked by a crudely built barricade. Two men climbed up the far side as they heard the cart. "Strangers are forbidden here!" one of them shouted.

"Why?" Grok called back.

"The church leaders have declared that the recent attacks are portents. The demons are sent to try us. Soon the Great One himself shall stand among us!"

"Why stop strangers?" Grok asked, in a friendly tone.

"The leaders say that strangers among us will dilute our holy spirits. If strangers pass through, the Great One will judge us unworthy of his presence. We will fall into barbarity like the heathens on the Isle of Skrelbard."

The skrel exchanged amused glances. "If you are civilized then I am proud to be a barbarian!" Grok shouted back, with a grin calculated to scare the men.

"And so it begins," muttered Calon Gan. Leku glanced at him. "When people are worried the churches see their chance," the old man said. "They force people to believe that some power will come to save them, if only they will do what they are told. The churches gain power and wealth. Their followers will commit atrocities in order to be saved. It has happened before, there is no use in talking."

There was a discussion among the men on the barricade. Then one of them shouted down. "The village of Eletlin is not far, they would not follow the Word. You heathens belong there."

The skrel made a collective decision to bypass the village. They were on the plains and so without difficulty, but some unavoidable damage to crops, they left the road and passed through fields. Once past Kelrith they rejoined the road and continued along it. Calon Gan tried to explain about Kelrith as they travelled. The level of blind obedience they had seen was alien to the Skrel.

"Many of these people are raised to obey authority; parents, priests, village leaders. It does things to their minds," Calon Gan told them. "They want to be told what to do. Especially when something like these demon attacks occur, they will obey without question."

The skrel shook their heads in amazement. "They do not ask questions?" asked Hauk.

"Questions are generally frowned upon."

The party travelled in relative silence until they reached the village of Eletlin. Some buildings had been burned, others were standing but abandoned to the elements. There were no bodies in the streets but scavengers, if not people, would have dealt with them.

"That is what they meant," said Thenk, surveying the ruined village.

"We should search the place and see if we can find anything useful," said Tharn.

As the group split up to search, Leku moved off

with Grok. "I need to be alone tonight."

"The full moon is tonight?" Grok asked him. Leku nodded. "Tharn knows. We will cover for you with the rest of them"

There was little enough in the village. As the skrel gathered around their cart, a group of soldiers on horseback rode up.

"Wait strangers! What is your business here?" their officer called.

"We are travellers. We came upon this village and stopped to investigate," said Thenk.

"This land is preparing for war. Grimevil is invading and all must account for themselves. You will accompany us until you are allowed to proceed with your business."

"Tornus Gan, stop being so stupid!" shouted Calon Gan.

Some turned to look at him. Grok, Leku and Hauk kept their eyes on the soldier, and were amused to see his expression slide from position of authority to embarrassed recognition.

"Uncle Calon," he said.

"Yes, Tornus. Your father told me you were doing well in the guard. Now tell us the news."

The soldiers were smirking at their officer's discomfort, he ignored them.

"Grimevil has invaded us. We are looking for any who may be their allies. We also have instructions to request help from any who may aid us."

"Do you have more equoths?" Calon Gan asked.

"Not far away, Uncle."

"Good, I am engaged on urgent business with three

of this party. The others have come south to aid in the fight, they can ride your extra equoths. If the Xetal do come through, they will be immune to possession and can help you.."

Tornus thought for a moment. "Do you wish to help us?" he asked the skrel.

"Yes," Hauk answered for the group.

"Our equoths can carry two for the short distance required. We must leave now," Tornus Gan told them.

The skrel rapidly said their goodbyes and mounted the equoths.

"Any message, Uncle?"

"Tell your parents that if all goes well, I will see them soon. If all does not go well, it will not matter. Goodbye, Tornus."

The equoths galloped off as Calon Gan and his skrel companions returned to their cart and the road ahead.

The sun was nearing the horizon as they stopped to camp for the night. Leku helped to prepare the camp and accepted some food. Before he left them, he spoke to Grok. "The fall of the barriers has altered the balance of this land. It will be difficult tonight."

Grok reached inside his shirt and pulled out the piece of bone that hung on the cord around his neck He lifted the cord over his head and gave it to Leku. "Take this, it might help," he told the werewolf.

Leku looked at it. The bone was polished, a picture of a wolf's head was carved and inked into it.

"Aula gave it to me, it has always been with me. If anything has my scent on it, that will," said Grok.

Leku continued to look at it. He was struck by the fact that Grok had remembered his sole mention of the visions of his friends helping him. Even more so by the fact that Grok would part, even briefly, with something that Aula had given him. He put it around his neck and, with a last look at Grok, walked off. Grok turned his attention back to the fire.

"Should we set up watches tonight?" Thenk asked.

"Leku was worried about the balance being disturbed. Then there may be more of those *pelcars* about," Grok said. "I think we should. I can take the first half."

"Wake me when you need to," Thenk told him.

"I am able to take a watch myself," Calon Gan told them.

"You should rest. We are more used to this life," Thenk said kindly.

"Very well, if I should wake early I will keep watch until we leave."

Calon Gan was on watch when a drawn and ruffled Leku returned to the camp. The werewolf sat down heavily by the fire. "The Council have brought the Xetal into the world," he said.

"Are you sure?"

"There are sources in the darkness. The Xetal have started to come through a portal. The Council had the Hammer of Colwen, they used two minor artefacts with it. They have all been absorbed into the Outer Darkness."

"That, at least, is good," Calon Gan said. "If none of the three major artefacts are left, no one else can use the Council's rite to call the Xetal." He looked across to where the other skrel were sleeping. "They should know. We must make haste to Barakelth," he said.

Leku woke his friends and told them the news as Calon Gan began to prepare breakfast. When Thenk moved to help the old man with the cooking, Leku took the bone from around his neck and handed it back to Grok. "Thanks," he said as he did so.

Grok nodded slightly as he looped the cord over his head.

They left their campsite and travelled along the road. The sun had passed its highest point when Calon Gan called Grok's name. The skrel turned to see him and saw the old man's eyes glaze over as he watched.

"What is it?" Grok asked.

Leku turned around to see them. "The Xetal, he's been possessed," he told Grok.

"Who are you?" growled Grok to Calon Gan's body.

"We have no names. We are who we are with no need of labels," Calon Gan's voice said.

"What do you want?" Thenk asked, having brought the cart to a halt.

"Why do you ask? I have possessed this man, I am part of an invading army. Why do you not attack?"

"That would involve killing Calon Gan. We are not prepared to do that," Thenk told the Xetal.

"But we expected..." the Xetal fell silent.

"You expected what?" growled Grok, in his most intimidating voice.

"It thought we would kill him," said Leku, slowly.

" Calon Gan dies, but what about the Xetal?" Grok

asked.

"You want to die. You are invading to die here," Leku said to the Xetal.

"They are here to die?" Thenk asked.

"Yes," replied the Xetal. "When last we entered your world, we discovered that those of us who possessed hosts died when the host body was destroyed. It was a revelation to us, to be able to end our existence. But we were driven back to our home and forced to continue our existence until we were called once more."

"Why do you want to die?" Leku asked it.

"We cannot cease on our plane. To never die, never sleep, ongoing consciousness for aeons. For long ages before your kind evolved, before life appeared on this world, we were aware. We will continue so unless we enter your plane and cease."

"How many of you are there?" Thenk asked.

"Many thousands, we all wish to cease."

"So that is why," muttered Grok. The others looked at him. "Some of the old stories from the war speak of warriors jumping off cliffs or not defending themselves in combat. No one ever knew why. Those Xetal wanted to die," he explained.

"You speak truly," the Xetal told him.

"But we cannot let you start a war just so you can die!" Grok growled.

"How will you stop us? Ceasing to exist is all we crave!"

Grok and Leku both growled menacingly at the Xetal.

"Death," muttered Thenk. "Death!" His friends both

jumped, and turned to look at him. "If we were able to offer all of you the chance to die, without a battle, would you accept?" Thenk asked the Xetal.

"All we wish for is non-existence."

"Leave this man and return at sunset. We will have a proposal for you then."

Calon Gan's body sagged as the Xetal left him. Grok caught him before he fell and gently laid him on the floor of the cart. Leku looked at Thenk.

"Yn Telkat an Relkat?" he asked.

"Yes," Thenk replied.

"We call Death and then what?" asked Grok.

"The Xetal want to die. If Death cannot help them, then maybe we can arrange it so they possess someone the moment before they die," Thenk told him.

"It will take time, but it could be done," said Leku.

"We call Death then."

"If he wants to come," Grok added. "We cannot insist, only ask."

Calon Gan assured them that he was recovered from his experience and stayed with the cart ,as the skrel moved from the road. They walked into a field and took up positions at the points of a triangle.

"I know the words," Grok said. "Thenk, when I finish the first run you join in. Leku, you come in on the third. If he hasn't come after ten rounds we give up." He took a breath.

"Gelth yn mort
Di henydd ul kaut
Fenris ulfr hel
Korangar korangar

Kalth kalth!"

Thenk joined in, then Leku. As they repeated the lines, a faint shape began to form between them. It solidified into a cowled figure that surveyed the skrel. "We meet again. That is most unusual," Death said.

"We have a question for you," said Thenk.

"What is it, Thenk al Krarg?"

"The Xetal are here, their only aim is to die. Can you help them?"

Death paused to consider matters. "Unless they possess a creature of this world I am unable to assist," he replied.

"Would it be possible for you to speak to them shortly before a suitable host dies? They could possess the host the instant before it dies, taking the Xetal with them," Thenk suggested.

"That will require work, but it is possible. Not all creatures are suitable, many will be sentient."

"That is why they must only be in possession an instant before the death."

"You are aware that no skrel can be possessed? Your people cannot be involved yet you ask others to be," Death said, looking at the three skrel.

"That is not a matter of choice for us," Thenk told him. "If this does not happen, then many will die in fighting between the Council, the Xetal and the rest of us. The Xetal will possess who they wish and force them to die. If you agree to our plan then the old, the sick and the mortally wounded will be possessed for an instant before their death. No one will be killed in order for the Xetal to die."

Death was silent as he pondered Thenk's speech.

"It will be done. All the Xetal must be on this world and their portal closed. They must spread over the world and each must wait for my message."

"Thank you. We will tell the Xetal," Thenk said.

"One more thing." Death turned to Grok. "You will not call me again."

Grok nodded. "We will meet again, but only once."

Death chuckled. "An amusing, yet fearsome, warrior. When shall we four meet again?" He faded from view.

"When shall we meet again?" asked Leku.

"It could be soon," said Thenk.

"We should take the Bror Oth," said Grok.

"To all meet the same fate?" asked Leku.

"It is very old, but the future is extremely uncertain."

"Agreed," said Leku.

"We will do it," said Thenk.

The three Skrel stood in a circle and joined hands. They stood silently for a moment and all began to recite.

"Earth, air and water,
Hear now the oath,
Of those skrel here.
As brothers, we will remain true,
Forever to defend the others,
To meet whatever fate awaits as one."

Chapter XXX

The Council were still en route to Barakelth. Tonb

had been looking unwell for some time, he collapsed and fell off his equoth. The other Council members stopped and surrounded him as he lay on the ground. He was having difficulty breathing, but he opened his eyes and looked at Geoe.

"So I am the sacrifice for Skallag's Bane," he whispered. "Go forth and do our duty."

Then he died, his body rapidly crumbling into dust.

Geoe pointed to another Councillor. "You, lead his horse. We continue to Barakelth."

The Lonskat of Grimevil was pacing on his balcony when the leader of the Geselftan came running up to him, trailed by a guard.

"Yes, Hilner?"

"Lonskat! I have great news! The energy source for the device has been renewed."

"You are able to bring the barriers down once more?"

"Yes. I have been experimenting since we last used the device. I believe it is possible to allow the magic through without demons being able to pass."

"So we would be able to use magic again?" the Lonskat asked.

"Yes, Lonskat. We could restrict the area of magic to Grimevil. We alone would have access to the power."

The Lonskat's mind teetered once more on the brink. "We would have the sole power?

"Yes. No one else but this land."

The mind lost its balance and fell into the abyss of insanity. "Do it, Hilner."

"Yes, Lonskat. It will take some time to prepare, I

will notify you." Hilner and the guard left, leaving the Lonskat to dream of power. To dream of a world without skrel spreading their ideas of all influencing leaders. A world where he would be immortal and lead the world forever. It would take time to bring the lands over the seas into his dominion, but he would have all the time in the world. So, the Glorious Cupric Age of Grimevil would begin.

Calon Gan was uneasy as sunset came nearer. He had not been aware of his possession by the Xetal, but it had left him with an unpleasant sensation in his head. The skrel had explained their plan to him and he had agreed, though he disliked the idea of being possessed again. They still had some way to go before reaching Barakelth but the roads could be difficult at night, so they planned to stop at a village they had seen in the distance.

Leku watched Calon Gan and offered his moral support. He alone of the groupl had an inkling of what the possession was like. Grok had slipped into the relaxed state of a long journey. He was lying in the back of the cart, using his pack as a pillow. His eyes were focused on infinity as his mind wandered the forests of Skrelbard.

"Grok!" Leku called.

"What is it?"

Leku pointed to Calon Gan. The old man's eyes were glazed; the Xetal was back.

"Thenk, stop," said Grok, urgently.

Thenk reined in the equoths and turned round to look at Calon Gan.

"I have returned," the old man's voice said.

"You will listen to our plan?" Thenk asked.

"I will."

"All the Xetal must pass through the portal immediately, then close it. They will then spread through the world. Death will tell you what you can possess and when. You will possess the host the instant before it dies, taking you with it."

"That will take time."

"What is that compared to your past?" Thenk asked.

"You insist the portal is closed?"

"Your portal endangers our world," Grok told him.

"That does not concern us."

"*Brak tel grach*!" Grok snarled at the old man.

Calon Gan's body shuddered, "You would do that?" the Xetal asked.

"If needs be," said Leku, ominously. He had no idea what Grok was talking about, but it seemed to be worrying the Xetal.

"The portal will be closed. In one of your hours," the Xetal decided.

"You accept our proposal?" Thenk asked.

"We do. Our," the Xetal paused, "thanks, go with you."

The Xetal departed as the skrel looked at each other.

At the ancient site, the portal glowed slightly in the fading light. Unseen, the Xetal flowed through in answer to the call from those already in the world. In the void beyond the portal a shape moved. Seemingly a simple sphere, yet in the next moment a many headed hydra, the thing drifted through the nothingness. Attracted to the energies of the portal, it moved to the hole in space and looked through. Before it could pass, the portal shrank to a pinprick and vanished.

Calon Gan was lying in the back of the cart as it rolled into the village. Leku sniffed the air. "The portal is closed," he told the others.

"Are we safe?" Thenk asked.

"Impossible to say. Anything could have come through. Grok, what was it you said to the Xetal?"

"I came across it in a manuscript when I was travelling with the Stone. A rite from this world the Xetal were afraid of. I have no idea how to do it."

Thenk glanced back at Calon Gan. "We should get him inside."

The village inn was small, but comfortable. Grok took some soup and bread to the room where Calon Gan was resting and joined his friends at the main table.

"Another day and we should be at Barakelth," said Thenk.

"What do we do if the Council get there first?" Leku asked.

"We fight." Thenk looked over at Grok's growled response. "This has to be ended soon," Grok continued.

Chapter XXXI

Hilner was working late in his workshop. The Lonskat had insisted that the apparatus had to be ready by morning. He was tired and somewhat worried about the Lonskat. That was probably why he made a mistake. He had realised that the minerals used in the apparatus prevented demons coming through, if enough minerals were present. He had solved that problem and was working on the placement of the mirrors. The mirrors had to be perfectly aligned for the barriers to fall solely in Grimevil. As he reached through the metal arms that supported the mirrors, he nudged one. It moved a fraction from its original position, enough to ruin the careful arrangements. Hilner continued working until he was satisfied the apparatus was prepared. He did not see the one mirror out of position.

Heavy cloud and rain obscured the sun completely when Calon Gan and the skrel left the inn the following morning. The same weather was heading to Barakelth as the ninety nine members of the Council continued their journey.

The sun was shining in Tolgath. Zen felt the warmth as he walked past a group of children playing in the centre of the village. Kris joined him as he walked to the Longhouse.

"Has there been any word from the south?" the young skrel asked.

"Very little, but I fear that events are moving too

fast for that. We will have to wait for their return in sunshine or in shadow."

"Until then we carry on. Drauk says his ale will be ready today. I have to help Ketha with the honey as well."

"Do not admit defeat until it is clear you are defeated," Zen muttered as Kris walked off.

Hilner fussed around his apparatus as the Lonskat walked in. He had taken a few hours sleep but he was still tired, hoping everything would work. The Lonskat was almost vibrating with energy this morning.

"It is ready Hilner?" he asked.

"Yes, Lonskat. I would suggest a very low level of energy first. These new settings are untried."

"Turn on the apparatus, Hilner. At full power."

"Lonskat?"

"Full power!"

Hilner paused, but his trust in, and fear of, the Lonskat won out and he pulled the switch. The apparatus started to glow and tremble slightly as Hilner stepped back to get an overall view. Both men could feel the power build-up as the energy filtered through the barriers. The Lonskat started to manipulate the energy, locating the Council far away. He formed a sphere of force and directed it towards them.

The first the Council knew of the matter was when one of them exploded in flames. Carmth of the Council had been schooled in magic and was a natural mage, he understood what had attacked them. He shouted a warning and tried to prepare a counterspell.

Hilner's mistake now revealed itself. Only the energies needed for magic were allowed through the barriers, but they were coming through at random points all over the world, not just in Grimevil. A potent flow of energy was filtering through near the Council. Carmth's relatively minor spell was boosted as it travelled along the magical trace to Grimevil and blasted the Lonskat. He stood up, smoking slightly, and prepared a devastating spell known to only a few of the old mages.

Geoe called to Carmth to block any further spells. The Councillor was casting at the same time as the Lonskat. Spell and counterspell met over northern Grimevil and shorted through the earth below.

No one was sure how many died in that cataclysm. The area was forever known as the blasted heath, nothing would grow there and the few trees that were not completely destroyed stood for many years, their twisted remains a mute monument to the tragedy. A witness to the events was Zen. A mirror in Tolgath was showing murky images of the encounter. Powerless to intervene, he watched as the struggle for power ended countless lives.

The Council had been forced to halt their journey, surrounded by a hemisphere of repelling force, they were safe. As the only way to be sure that the attacks had ceased was to leave the hemisphere, no one had moved. A certain amount of arguing was going on but they stayed inside.

The Lonskat was pacing up and down near the

device. He was alone, Hilner had fled when Carmth's spell had entered the room. The Lonskat had seen what the Council had done and was determined to break their shield. Working on a powerful spell, he concentrated it into a beam of force directed at the Council. Knowing that he was omnipotent, he waited for their shield to collapse.

The beam of force reached the shield and was repelled. It was reflected back along the route it had taken. The Lonskat was still anticipating the success of his plan when he was vapourised by the magic.

Some time later, when some of the Lonskat's staff timidly entered the room, they found no trace of their leader. The only thing in the room was the charred and tangled wreckage of Hilner's apparatus.

Chapter XXXII

Hauk, Tharn and their group of skrel and humans were attacked by Grimevillian forces, as their compatriots were nearing Barakelth. They were only a small group, but fortunately they were not outnumbered by their attackers.

Tharn was swinging his axe, causing the Grimevillians to keep their distance, and found himself fighting next to Tornus Gan. He cleaved the sword arm from an enemy attempting to stab Tornus and felt a sword cut into his own arm. Tornus' blade sliced through the air and buried itself in the neck of his attacker.

Ignoring the pain, Tharn nodded to Tornus and

carried on fighting. The skirmish continued for a few bloody minutes more, then all the Grimevillians lay around them, dead. The Corbusians and skrel were injured with two seriously hurt. Tharn ran to where Hauk was lying, surrounded by the rest of the skrel. His breathing was shallow and he opened his eyes to look at the ring of faces around him. His gaze stopped at Tharn.

"Make sure Thenk is successful, do not let the Council win,"he said. His eyes closed and the skrel heard the death rattle in his throat.

"He died saving me," said Kauth. He raised his head and shouted. "*Ket malth, ton dikelch!*"

The others joined in, the lament for the one killed echoing from the hills.

Later, they were finishing Hauk's pyre when Tornus spoke to Tharn. "Tel Dormun has just died. He fought bravely alongside you."

"He deserves the Thor Valk, as do all who die fighting the Council," Tharn told him.

The two bodies were placed on the pyre and it was lit. As the flames rose, the skrel moved slowly round repeating the chant to honour the dead.

"*Orc tell brach,*
Orc bern orth arcon rof cynan.
Calt grat, ran crof thrunkal,
Throm tel, brach skrel."

When the humans had memorised the words, they joined in. The words rose with the smoke into the sky.

Calon Gan had recovered by the time they reached

Barakelth. A friend of his lived nearby, if he was still there. He drew his breath in sharply as he saw the house. It had been badly damaged and there was no sign of anyone. Thenk brought the cart to a halt outside and Calon Gan called out. "Telon! Are you here?"

After a pause the battered door opened a fraction, then it opened fully and a middle aged man emerged.

"Calon Gan! Come inside, the equoths can be stabled around the back," he said.

"What news, Telon?"

"Demons have been attacking for some time. The days are safe, not so the nights. What brings you here?"

"The Council of Barakelth. Do you know of the Pyramid of Khelton Leveth?"

"Yes, I have heard of it."

"How do you use it?" growled Grok, ever practical.

"The base has an inscription in magic runes," Telon told him. "They will appear in any language you know. You must speak the words aloud, then the Pyramid will act against the Council of Barakelth."

"Do you know where it is?" Calon Gan asked his friend.

"A cave, near here. The exact location is unknown, there may be magic protecting the Pyramid which makes it difficult to find."

Darkness was nearing, and on the advice of Telon they decided to stay at his house. Any demon attacks stood a chance of affecting the Council if they were in the area, so they would be camped defensively instead of holding ceremonies.

The group had eaten and were preparing to sleep, when the demons attacked. As tall as Telon, armed with long fangs and claws, they burst into the house. Leku pushed Calon Gan into a small side room as he picked up a club. Telon was nearer the door and had no time to hide. He grabbed a solid staff and swung at the demons. One casually threw out an arm, scoring a wound down his arm.

Now armed, the skrel attacked the demons. Even with gouges in their flesh the demons kept attacking. Grok was only wearing his cloth shirt and a claw caught his chest, tearing open his skin. As Grok stumbled, Telon's staff cracked the creature's skull. The demon turned to this new attacker, allowing Thenk to cleave its head from its neck, but not before its claw had severed Telon's jugular.

Leku's club broke the arm of another creature as Grok regained his balance. Grok's axe rose and fell, burying itself in a fiend's skull as Thenk killed the last remaining creature.

Ignoring the blood soaking into his shirt, Grok went to help Telon, but the man was beyond his aid. The human tried to speak as Grok raised him from the floor. "*Orc tell am gremnor, calt grat,*" Grok said gently. Telon lifted a hand and clasped the arm that held him, then he died. The skrel looked at his friends. "He has gone."

Calon Gan emerged and looked at his dead friend. "So many deaths," he whispered.

Leku left the room for a moment and returned with a glass of the potent Frelet spirit, which he gave to the old man.

"Thor Valk?" the werewolf asked his friends. They nodded.

As Leku and Thenk left the room Grok pulled his shirt off to examine the wound on his chest. It was not deep, but it was bleeding profusely. Grok pulled a dressing from his pack and applied it as Calon Gan spoke to him. "Thor Valk?"

"A special rite. The body of one who has died is burned, as is our custom, but with the chant of Thor Valk. It is the highest honour we have for the dead. Those who have died defending others are the only ones who receive it. Telon was helping to defend us."

None of the group slept well that night. Telon's death added to the feeling of despair that they tried to keep away. During the night, unable to sleep, Thenk left the room where they were quartered and moved to the main room. Grok was already there, looking out at Telon's pyre. The skrel had used the woodpile stored for winter, and added some of the damaged timbers from the house with lamp oil. The fire lit up Grok's face as he softly recited the words of the Thor Valk. He looked around as Thenk joined in.

"The Thor Valk is still an honour even if it does not last until the pyre is gone," Thenk said.

"How is Calon Gan?" asked Grok, as he turned from the window.

"Sleeping. It was a bad shock, but he is a tough one."

"If we get out of this, we have to get him home safely."

Thenk nodded. "He did not have to come with us. I

think his life has been calmer than any of ours."

"It ends tomorrow. The end of the Council or of us."

Chapter XXXIII

As the sun rose, Geoe and Chene surveyed Barakelth, home of the Council. They were standing on top of a small rise, looking down at the ruins of the old Council Chamber. Below, Councillors were just waking to prepare for the most important day of their lives. They had been delayed by the Lonskat's attack. When the Inner Council had tired of waiting, they pushed a lesser member out of the protective hemisphere. Seeing that he came to no harm, they continued the journey.

"You have memorised the ritual?" Geoe asked.

"I have," Chene told him.

"Good, always two must know it."

"One more thing," she said, moving closer.

Geoe made a slight noise and crumpled to the ground. Chene looked at him dispassionately, the blade of her knife stained red.

"Only two can know. I told Terob yesterday."

She turned and went to join the other Councillors.

Thenk had fed and watered the equoths, then joined the others outside the house. The pyre was still smouldering as they left. The skrel scanned the area for any signs of a cave. There were no obvious signs but the landscape lent itself to caves, the area was thickly wooded and full of hollows. They decided to split up and search. Whichever group found the cave would make a drafan call.

Grok and Leku moved off, walking quietly into the trees and undergrowth. The woods were at their most lush and the wildflowers added colour and scent to the scene, an incongruous setting for the evil of the Council. Thenk looked over to Calon Gan.

"You can wait here while I search."

"No. We must make all speed to find the Pyramid. Too many people have died for us to fail now."

They walked into the trees opposite to the direction taken by Grok and Leku, looking for anything that could conceal the mouth of a cave.

Chene looked over the assembled Council. This was her moment, the time she had been dreaming of for fifty years.

"Our leader Geoe has been struck down at the moment of our triumph. His killers must be nearby still. Some of you must search for them. The rest of us will prepare for the final ceremony. *Libet, sepon, hainess!*"

A few of the Councillors left as the others arranged burners of herbs and hung small banners.

A slight rustling in the undergrowth was all the noise made by the skrel as they searched.

"Do caves smell different when you are outside?" asked Grok.

"Not really," Leku replied. "I am no help there. We just have to look everywhere. The entrance is probably hidden well."

They continued in silence for some time until a crashing noise ahead stopped them. It was a human, not making any attempt to be quiet. Any human in this place acting like that was probably from the Council, the skrel reached for their weapons.

The human caught sight of them as he passed through the trees. He screamed as he charged at them. The skrel held their ground and Grok's axe and Leku's club swung together. Between them, the weapons sent the man to the ground mortally wounded.

Grok silently bent down and used his axe to end the man's life swiftly. The Skrel did not believe in allowing anyone to slowly and painfully bleed to death, not even their worst enemies. Better that the death be quick. As he rose, a large chunk of stone hit his forehead causing him to fall to the ground. Leku turned to the place where the stone had come from and hefted his club as a figure emerged, brandishing a sword.

"An elf! I should have realised from the rotten scent."

"The bestial skrel! Chene did not say you had to be alive. You will be the first. Soon the world will be free of Skrel."

Leku was slowly circling, bringing the elf between himself and Grok. The elf seemed amused. "Scared, skrel?"

"You do not know, do you? None of you realise the danger."

"The elves know everything!"

"Even what will happen when you destroy the Skrel?"

"The world will be a cleaner place!"

"Come on then. Start! I will make it easier." Leku threw his club to one side.

"That will not help you," said the elf, as he changed his grip on the sword.

"You would kill an unarmed skrel?" growled a voice behind him.

The elf turned to see a skrel with blood covering his face, eyes and teeth shining. The last thing he heard was Grok's roar as he charged.

The Council were assembled and silent. The burners were sending the aroma of herbs into the air. Chene stood in front of them, flanked by the Inner Council.

"Now is the day of our destiny. The Council of Barakelth stands once more ready to rule. Our allies the Xetal will soon join us in battle. We will be invincible. Now begins a new era, the reign of the Council!"

She began to speak the words to release the Council's power. All who wore the sign of the Council would be able to pierce the barriers and tap the energies of the Outer Darkness. They would become mages of darkness, possessed of incalculable power. With no mages to oppose them this time, they would be unstoppable.

"Thanks," said Leku.

"Enemies are easy to find, good friends are rare."

Grok bent down to the headless body and searched it. He pulled a medallion from it and showed it to Leku.

"Council member."

"We need to find that pyramid. These two will be found soon," said the werewolf. "Leave them here. They will become part of what they would have destroyed."

Thenk and Calon Gan moved slowly through the wood, looking for indications of a cave. Thenk glimpsed a dark portal behind some foliage and pulled the plants aside, revealing the entrance to a small cave. Glancing at Calon Gan, he walked in. The cave was not big. He paused to light a torch and explored it. The floor was sandy and dry, there were no tracks apart from those of small animals. Calon Gan followed him in and, at the back of the cave on a small pedestal, they saw the Pyramid of Khelton Leveth. It was made of polished gold and the light from the torch reflected from it as they looked.

"Just sitting here? No traps?" Thenk whispered.

"I suspect that magic was placed on there many years ago. If anyone tried to move it from its position, some magical trap would be triggered." Calon Gan realised he was also whispering and raised his voice. "We should not touch it, just read the inscription."

"I will call the others."

Thenk wedged his torch into a crevice, then moved back to the mouth of the cave and a drafan hoot echoed around. He returned to Calon Gan, who was studying the Pyramid by the light of the torch.

"Do we need all of us to be here?"

"I do not think so. We just need to read the inscription on the edges." He peered at the bottom of the pyramid and began to speak.

Grok and Leku looked at each other as they heard the familiar call of a drafan.

"This way," Leku said, as he hurried south, in the direction of the call.

The six Councillors from the group Chene had sent out also heard the call.

"Wait," said one, holding up his hand. "That was a signal."

"No," said another. "It was just some bird."

"It was a drafan call," the other told him. "I have heard them along the north coast of Erein."

"So?"

"They do not live here. Someone from the north is here, using it as a signal. Now, follow me."

In the ruins of Barakelth, Chene continued to speak. The Council nearing their goal, were unaware of the efforts being made to stop them.

Calon Gan finished speaking. Nothing happened. Thenk glanced at him.

"I do not understand," the old man said, "that should have been enough. You should try reading the inscription."

As Thenk glanced at the symbols on the Pyramid, he felt the words come into his mind. He began to speak as Calon Gan moved to the mouth of the cave. The old man saw Grok and Leku approaching and as they reached him Thenk reappeared, shaking his head.

"You have found the Pyramid?" Leku asked.

"Yes, but we cannot use it. We read the inscription with no result," said Calon Gan.

There was a volley of stones from slings that sent Calon Gan to the ground, blood running from his head. The skrel formed a protective line in front of him. The Councillors reached the skrel and attacked. Leku's club knocked one senseless. Grok's axe swung alongside him, parrying a blow from a Councillor's sword. Thenk's sword reached under the guard of another and slashed open the man's chest. The Councillor swung wildly at Grok who easily dodged the blow. He brought his axe down and severed the man's sword arm at the elbow. The man screamed as the limb fell to the ground. He stopped as Grok's axe cleaved his neck. Grok felt the wound from the previous night open again as he attacked. Beside him, Leku's club broke a human's arm, allowing the werewolf to club him senseless. Leku's face showed fierce concentration, unlike his friends, he could not allow bloodlust to rise. That way lay darkness. Thenk, once more getting under his enemy's guard, stabbed the man with his sword. The weapon pierced the Councillor's back, Thenk tugged it free as a woman swung a rapier at him. His first blow caused her to stagger back. Thenk glanced at Grok's bloodied face and shouted, "The Pyramid!" before returning to the fray.

Grok ducked inside the cave as the two remaining attackers tried to flee. Leku and Thenk chased after them, keeping them from the cave and Calon Gan. Grok took a moment to allow his eyes to adjust to the torchlight and crossed to the Pyramid on its pedestal. Just as Calon Gan had said, there were symbols on the lower edges. He looked at them, and saw them flow and change into the Skrellian language. He took a breath.

"Orc yl croesen nul
Arel yn tayr
Ar y reln yt y Skrel
Arel grat!"

For a moment there was silence. Then with a faint hissing noise, the Pyramid seemed to blossom. The sides unfolded, revealing a dazzling light, as Grok stepped back.

A huge wind erupted from it. The gust lifted Grok off his feet and blew him out of the cave. As he crashed to the ground, it continued out, plucking the Councillors from the ground as they ran from the skrel. It briefly swirled, indecisively, before moving to where the Council were gathered in the ruins. They were still chanting the rite to put themselves in contact with the Outer Darkness as the gale burst upon them. A howling, tearing wind that lifted them from the ground, their screams mingled with the screaming of the wind. The chant faded as the Councillors tried to run away.

"No!" screamed Chene. "We must make contact! We can defeat this!"

His cloak flapping around him violently, Terob held on to a wall as he tried to continue the incantation. " *Un pace de teum parla. Pace, pace, tarandanus brachyurus. Por el...*" The wind pulled him into the air, sucking the breath from his lungs.

The wind kept the Councillors aloft, many unable to take a breath. Some screams echoed around the ruins as Chene tried to continue chanting. "*Por el cave non erat lare meum.* No!" she screamed, her face contorted in anger as the wind plucked her into the air.

With its burden of Councillors, the wind raced back to the cave and into the Pyramid. When the last figure had vanished inside, the sides folded back and concealed the light. Its purpose completed, the dull and tarnished Pyramid toppled off the pedestal.

Then there was silence. As Leku and Thenk moved back to the cave, they saw leaves stripped from the trees by the passage of the wind fall gently on the still forms of Grok and Calon Gan.

Chapter XXXIV

When Grok opened his eyes again, he saw a shaft of sunlight streaming through a window. It faded as a cloud obscured the sun before reappearing. He realised he was lying in a bed. As he sat up, the sheet fell from his chest revealing new bandages over the wound the demon had inflicted. The dressing he had used had been replaced and the hair was no longer matted with blood. He saw his possessions in various places around the room.

As he tried to call out, he realised how dry his throat was. A jug of water stood by the bed. He sniffed it cautiously and drained it before trying to call again.

"Hey! Anyone home?"

There was a pause and then he heard footsteps outside. The latch rattled and the door swung open to reveal Calon Gan. He smiled when he saw Grok sitting up.

"You are back with us at last."

"At last?"

"You have been asleep for almost two days. We are in Telon's house. Leku and Thenk brought you back here from the cave. You succeeded. The Council has been destroyed."

"How are you?"

"I am feeling my years, but I am well enough. Leku thinks you have two or three cracked ribs, but otherwise you are just battered about."

He crossed the room and sat on the end of the bed. Grok moved to give him room and winced as everything except his feet protested.

"Unfortunately, we were not quite fast enough. Magic energy is leaking through the barriers, thus, the level of available magic is considerably increased."

"What does that mean?"

"Life will be different. The Freidyn scholars were correct when they said that the Skrel would be important, but they looked no farther forward. We have no guides for the future."

Grok rubbed a hand against his beard. "Why did the Pyramid only work for me?"

"Thenk and Leku have been investigating the Council Chambers. I have been reading Telon's books for information. We have only one source, yet it seems that Khelton Leveth created the Pyramid so that only a person of a certain type could use it. The Councillors are not empathic people nor do they value the lives of others. The Pyramid was designed so that any of the Council or their ilk could not release its power. The only person who could is one who not only values and feels for others, but has experienced the death of one very close to them. The source does state that Khelton Leveth never fully recovered from the loss of his wife in an attack by the Council. I would speculate that the only one of us who is not fully reconciled to the death of a loved one, is you."

Grok's eyebrows drew together as he looked at Calon Gan suspiciously.

"You father-in-law told me of Aula and Krarg," the old man said. "He also told me of your duel with Death. Your wife, your son and your unborn child were snatched away from you. My wife, Catha, was taken by a fever. I had time to prepare myself for her death and I have had many years to deal with her loss. You have had less than three years to deal with yours. I suspect that I know the method used to destroy the Spear of Pyra and the burden you took upon yourself. You could never allow one of your friends to take that burden."

Grok's eyes were fixed on Calon Gan's face. The old man ignored the piercing gaze and continued speaking.

"You were the one who Khelton Leveth wanted to use the Pyramid, whether he knew it or not. If not you, it would be someone like you. Someone not reconciled to a death. Of all of us here, only you could release the power of the Pyramid. Because you are the only one who has paid the price demanded."

Later, when Leku looked in on Grok, he was sleeping again. As the werewolf looked at his friend's face, he could see that his dreams were not pleasant.

Over supper that night the three discussed their plans.

"Now that Grok is recovering, I would like to return home as soon as I can," said Calon Gan.

"So do we," Leku told him.

"What will you do?" asked Thenk.

"Rest, speak with the few Freidyn left."

"There is more the Freidyn can do for the world. They can recruit more members."

"More Freidyn?"

"Yes. The Freidyn have faded as the magic faded. The world will have need of you again. You and the rest of the Freidyn must pass on your knowledge to younger members before it is lost and the Freidyn disappear."

"There is truth in what you say. New members of the Freidyn can learn from us and then learn more."

"None of us know what will happen with wild magic but no mage guilds to control it. The Freidyn will be needed once more."

Unsettled, Leku woke before dawn. Leaving Gan and Thenk to sleep, he padded to the room where Grok was, to check on him. Grok was sitting by the window looking out at the darkness. As Leku entered, he turned to the door. "I am not the only one awake then," he said.

"Did Calon Gan tell you about the Pyramid?" Leku asked.

"Yes, he told me what he read."

"Did he tell you why he thinks that you, not himself or Thenk was successful?" Grok nodded. "I think he is right, Khelton Leveth may not have known that his grief was passed into the spells he cast. Just as you think none of us know how you feel about your family." The werewolf ignored the sharp look Grok gave him as he continued, "We did not tell him about the Spear. I think he knows us well enough to reason out how it was destroyed."

"Possibly he does," Grok growled. "It seems that people know more than I think."

There was a silence.

"How are you, Grok?"

"In pain."

"No, I mean you."

"The Pyramid needed sorrow, regret and grief. It got them from me. Now I know what Zen meant about regrets."

Leku waited but Grok did not elaborate.

"All werewolves know that sometimes bad things happen to people for no reason. We exist by no fault of our own, we did not choose to become werewolves. But if you had not destroyed the Spear, you would not be the friend I know. What makes a skrel is not just the choices he makes, but how he lives with them."

"Zen?"

"No. Leku."

The werewolf was pleased to see his friend

laughing in the pre-dawn light.

They left Telon's house later that morning and arrived in Penmin several days later on a pleasant summer evening. Grok went to collect Zehc as the others unloaded packs and aired Calon Gan's house. The black and white dog was overjoyed to see Grok again and kept jumping up to lick him. He thanked the friend of Calon Gan who had taken care of his dog and walked back to meet his friends.

They ate at an inn and took a small barrel of local beer back to Calon Gan's house. They sat outside in the evening sunshine with Zehc lying on Grok's feet, the better to know if the skrel was moving from his seat.

"The Council have been defeated, hopefully so has Grimevil," said Thenk, helping himself to more beer.

"What has happened to Tharn and his friends?" Leku asked the world in general.

"We might need to wait until we reach Skrelbard to hear about them."

"How do we get back there, *Gremnor?*" Leku asked Grok.

"The best way is by sea," Grok told him, grinning at Thenk. "By land will take far longer. We should see which ships are leaving soon."

"Is there another way to hear about what happened in the battles with Grimevil," Thenk wondered.

"I do have a means of talking to other towns by way of magic," Calon Gan said, hearing Thenk's comment as he joined them, "but I do not know who has the necessary mirrors. That will be more work for the Freidyn. Many people who have the mirrors may be unaware of their power."

The following day, Grok and Leku took Zehc out along the cliffs while Thenk walked down into the village to learn about sailing times. He was told that a boat would be leaving for Grimsbal in two days and one for Execrul in four days. He decided to take the second boat, since the sea journey would be shorter and they could go overland from Execrul to Grimsbal and then to Skrelbard.

Before the Skrel left Penmin, Gan was able to contact Zen by mirror. They learned from him about the disaster on the blasted heath and some news from Tharn. The skrel had located a working mirror and told Zen of Grimevil's defeat.

"We must remember," said Thenk. "No one else will."

The ship for Execrul was preparing to leave as the skrel and Calon Gan arrived at Penmin's harbour. Grok was carrying letters for members of the Freidyn along their route. All of them were uncertain what to say.

Calon Gan finally broke the silence. "We are taking your advice and recruiting to the Freidyn, those letters will notify other members. Our knowledge may be needed again and we need younger people to travel for us."

"Remember to visit Skrelbard, there will be young skrel who can help you," said Thenk.

"I will."

"We should go," said Grok. "We will meet again, Calon Gan." He walked up the gangplank and onto the ship, Zehc following him.

"He always make a farewell short," said Thenk.

They took longer to bid farewell to the old man, then boarded the ship.

Calon Gan waved as the ship moved away from its moorings. When it reached the headland, he turned and began to walk home. There was work to do.

A number of weeks later, they sat around a campfire at the Pass of Gronman.

"And so it ends," said Thenk. "Tomorrow we reach home."

"This anyway. You heard Calon Gan. Things will change," Leku commented, reaching to scratch Zehc behind the ears.

The dog had taken to travelling well. If he was with Grok, he was happy.

"There is still wood to cut, animals to hunt," Grok said.

"And demons?"

"Maybe," said Leku. "The barriers have been weakened, but things are not as bad as I feared. We know the artefacts have been destroyed; that is good. No one can safely contact the Outer Darkness without them. Calon Gan told me that the Council all bore a certain mark on their bodies. Without that mark, contact would be dangerous."

"Humans are very strange creatures," Grok growled. "There would be some who would try."

"Very little can be certain for now."

As they entered Tolgath, they suddenly halted as they saw what had happened to the village. Two houses were missing and part of the Longhouse was being rebuilt.

"What happened here?" whispered Thenk.

"We need to see Zen."

They hurried to the Longhouse and the aged skrel came out to meet them, smiling broadly.

"You return to us safe and well. Tharn returned yesterday. Hauk of Tromok died in Corbus."

"What happened here?"

"Demons attacked. The family of Herok y Telth was killed. Dak died driving the demons away. Others were hurt."

The travellers were silent, absorbing Zen's news. Zehc, not concerned, pushed his nose into Zen's hand, knowing that the skrel would pet him.

"As before, when the Council were defeated, demons attacked," Zen continued, stroking Zehc. "Once again we have magic to help defeat them. We must have a feast now that all our wanderers have returned."

That evening they had a quiet meal with Zen and told him what had happened at Barakelth. They talked of Telon's death and the Pyramid of Khelton Leveth. When Grok did not reveal the details of who had used the Pyramid and why, his friends stayed silent. If Grok was not talking about it, neither would they.

They had heard more news on their journey to Skrelbard. Grimevil was in turmoil. With the Lonskat dead, many others were fighting to take his place as ruler. The deaths on the heath were blamed on the Council. No one fully understood what had happened and the Council was a useful scapegoat.

The Council's deal with the Caran Church had come to light and many clergy had fled in fear of their lives. There had been stories of churches being attacked by mobs, furious that their religious leaders had sided with a group that had caused the deaths of their own followers in demon attacks.

"The world will be different," Zen said.

Preparations for the feast began early the next day. One or two older skrel who made comments that a werewolf would not be welcome at the feast were immediately quelled by one glare from Grok.

"It is a good thing Grok is not a mage," said Kris, observing one of them hurrying away from his friend.

"How exactly?" asked Thenk.

"He can scare Jarn like that just by looking. Imagine what would happen if he had magic backing it up."

It was a feast for those returned and those never to return. Deer, boar, grouse and more were served. Bards sang and poems were recited. Some time after the food was consumed, while the entertainment was continuing, Grok silently slipped outside. Zen followed him and found him looking up at the stars.

"I just needed some time," Grok growled.

"I understand. One only needs to look in your eyes to see that you are not the same skrel who left."

For the only time in his life, Grok spoke of the destruction of the Spear of Pyra. Zen closed his eyes as the young skrel gruffly told him what had happened and put a hand on Grok's shoulder.

"Your grandfather once told me you were a *thararn*, he was right. Few skrel could have done what you did," He paused. "The bards are asking for details of your travels."

Grok's eyes turned to look at him. "Tell them a werewolf helped save them. Tell them of the deaths."

Zen nodded, understanding Grok's meaning. He turned and walked back into the Longhouse. Left alone, Grok felt a nudge on his leg. He looked down into the soft brown eyes of Zehc.

"Come on then."

They walked back into the Longhouse. The noise of skrel enjoying themselves and the light of the lamps spilled out into the night, as the moon shone placidly down over Skrelbard.